# The Teacher

# And

# Puddin' Head

**Joe R. Tueller**

Copyright © 2003 by Joseph R. Tueller

ISBN  0-7414-1603-4

Cover Art: Montana Prairie by Annie Olander

*Published by:*

PUBLISHING.COM

*519 West Lancaster Avenue*
*Haverford, PA 19041-1413*
*Info@buybooksontheweb.com*
*www.buybooksontheweb.com*
*Toll-free  (877) BUY BOOK*
*Local Phone (610) 520-2500*
*Fax  (610) 519-0261*

*Printed in the United States of America*

*Printed on Recycled Paper*

*Published  July 2003*

# Dedication

To Kristine:
Truly a daughter for all seasons

# 1

Land sakes but he's big!

That thought came into Emily's head even before she wondered what he wanted in her classroom. He carefully pushed open the door and his form filled the entire door frame. She judged him to be not much more than twenty years old so he couldn't be one of the town School Board members stopping in to monitor her class work. If he was a cowboy, he wasn't dressed for the range—not with those store-bought britches, shirt and black string necktie. Even his boots were shined. Since she had met most of the townspeople, she was quite sure he wasn't one of them.

He meant to make his entry unobtrusive, but failed miserably. Although he ducked for the doorway, he misjudged the height and had his hat knocked off. Whirling to catch it, he collided with the door, slamming that heavy, double-planked member against the inner wall of the log building with a percussion that brought even the most lethargic student into shocked awareness. As heads turned in unison, one spur caught in a floorboard crack and would have sent him sprawling if he hadn't made a desperate grab for the door frame and hung on. While locked in that position, flushed and with perspiration showing on his untanned forehead, he reluctantly lifted his gaze to meet the fifteen pairs of eyes that watched in stunned silence.

It was Frida Anderson, a lively ten-year old, who finally broke the spell. Pointing at the unfortunate interloper, she broke into shrieking, wild laughter. That was joined by outbursts of one youngster after another until pandemonium ensued.

The teacher tried vainly to restore order until the absurdity of the whole situation overwhelmed her and she covered her mouth to hide her mirth. Emily O'Neill, graduate of Smith College, class of 1888, she said to herself, what are you doing so far from New york watching a clumsy lummox trying to break his neck in the tiny schoolhouse of Broken Wagon, Montana? She collected herself and was about to start forward to see if she could provide assistance, but with a supreme effort he tore loose the spur and, with it, a long splinter of wood from the floor. Then he stood and glared at the frolicking class. Each member, singled out by a stare that carried with it the horror of the unknown, became suddenly quiet until there was complete silence in the room.

Emily watched, fascinated. Finally she cleared her throat and said, "Is there something I can do for you Mister ...?" She waited for him to provide a name.

Frida spoke first. "That's Puddin' Head," she announced proudly.

"Frida!" the teacher admonished.

"Well, that's what everybody calls him— Puddin' Head Jones." She partly covered her mouth and whispered to her seatmate, Mary, "Wooden Head, Puddin' Head Jones," and both girls giggled.

Almost everyone heard, of course, and the giggling became contagious. "Class, that's quite enough!" The teacher's voice had risen another octave. "...And you, Frida, I'll speak to you after school. Now I'm sure that's not Mister...Jones' name." She gave him a questioning look.

"No ma'am," he said glaring at Frida. "It's..." He hesitated for a moment. Then his face brightened with recollection. "Andrew. Andrew Jones."

"Very well, Mister Jones, would you please tell me why you're here." Her tone suggested that she was becoming a trifle impatient.

"Ma says I hafta go to school." When that brought forth snickers and chuckles, he glared at the class and added, "Ain't my idee."

"But aren't you a little...old?" She said gently. She had started to say "big".

"Ma says she pays school tax so she gits to send one of hers. I'm the youngest so I'm the one. Don't like it one bit."

Emily wondered how his mother could make that big clod do anything. "This is very unusual." She wished there was someone who could give her advice in dealing with the matter. "What grade would you be in, Mister Jones?"

"Dunno," he answered. "Ain't never been to school." Again the snickers.

"Land sakes! Why not?"

"Pa says I don't need it."

"And now he's changed his mind?"

"He's dead."

"Oh, I'm sorry." She truly was sorry. The young man looked like he needed a father to whom he could turn for guidance. He certainly didn't seem to have control of his life. "Very well," she said at last. "Please take a seat next to Mister Vik." Puddin' Head knew Alf Vik's youngest son, Hans.

The students were seated on benches next to tables—both types of furniture had been hand-hewn from logs. Unfortunately the pieces were intended to accomodate children and had not been sized to fit someone of Puddin' Head's dimensions. He sat with his knees at armpit level. Heads turned to observe his discomfort. The girls giggled with their heads together—the boys nudged each other and smirked.

Puddin' Head glowered as Emily handed him slate, chalk and a wipe cloth. "Now then, class, let's begin."

The eight boys and six girls that made up the class ranged in age from seven to fifteen. That and the wide variation in educational backgrounds made the teacher's job particularly challenging. Emily was trying to group her students according to their ability in several subjects. That tactic was not completely successful and was now further complicated by the big man sitting at the back of the room.

She consulted her notes. "Judith, Olav and Jacob, continue your longhand practice of letters 'J', 'K' and 'L'. Don't wipe your slates until I can look at your work.

"Melba and Edria, I want you to read together chapter three in the primer. Get started—I'll help you in a few minutes. Sven, Oskar, Arne and Henry—multiplication for numbers seven and eight. Frida, Mary and Tom—the story on page thirty-eight. Betsy and Hans, your history assignment for this week will be the Roman Empire. You're going to be asked to write a brief summary."

Now Mister Jones, she thought. He was sitting there looking at her with that scowl on his face. Doesn't he ever smile, she wondered. If he tried, he might be fairly handsome—certainly has nice blue eyes. Strong jaw line. Fair complexion—must be part Swede. I suppose I'd better get on with this.

As she approached he tried to get to his feet as he'd seen gentlemen do. In the process he almost tipped over the bench. Hans grabbed for the table knocking his book to the floor.

"No!" she said in alarm. "Please stay seated."

Henry Gibbons got into a laughing fit which stopped abruptly when Emily yelled at him in a shrill voice. After some semblance of order had been restored she turned again to Puddin' Head. "I want to ask you some questions." She spoke quietly hoping the class would get back to work. The quick glances that came her way told her that something less than total dedication to their studies was taking place. She sat on the bench and leaned close so that only he could hear her words. "Do you know your letters?"

"Yup," he answered. He had one of those big, outdoor voices that was impossible to attenuate. "My brother, Henrik told me—aye, bee, cee...," he began reciting. That set off a chorus of suppressed giggles."

"Never mind," she whispered quickly. Then aloud, "Class, will you please give all of your attention to your assignments. My discussion with Mister Jones is none of your concern."

She turned back to Puddin'head. "Can you spell any words?"

"My name."

"Your name. Anything else?"

"Cat."

Hans, on Puddin' Head's other side, snorted.

"Mister Vik," she scolded, "if you haven't enough to do I can certainly give you some extra assignments that you can do at home."

Puddin' Head added his scowl to her comments. Hans looked properly chastised.

"Cat," she repeated. "That's it?"

He shrugged, embarrassed.

"Well," she said, feeling slightly ill, "and your figures?"

"Huh?"

"Your figures—numbers? Can you count?"

"Huh?" Puddin' Head was being distracted by the teacher who leaned toward him until their shoulders touched. He could smell the faint scent of lilac about the young woman and knew it was one of the most exciting sensations he had ever experienced. When she talked, she bobbed her head slightly so that her reddish-brown curls bounced. Puddin' Head was enchanted.

"Can you hear me?" she said, exasperated.

"Uh...yes ma'am."

"Well?"

Her question finally registered with him. "Yes ma'am. I can count." He decided not to demonstrate.

"Can you do arithmetic?"

"Arith...?"

"Addition, subtraction."

"Uh...little bit."

"Multiplication? Division?"

He shook his head.

Emily sat upright and looked at him for a long period of time, thinking, until he began to fidget under her scrutiny. Finally she leaned near him again, keeping her voice low, "Mister Jones, I will have to start you at the bottom of the class. Are you sure you want to do this?"

He seemed uncertain. "Ma says I hafta."

She sat away from him again and sighed.

"Very well," she told him quietly. Do the exercise I assigned to Judith, Olav and Jacob. Practice the letters I've written on the blackboard. Later I'll give you some other letters so you can catch up."

She noticed, then, that nearly everyone in the class was openly watching. They quickly ducked their heads over their slates and books when she stood. This will never do, she decided.

When school ended that day, Puddin' Head had been working on his letters except for those periods of time when he surreptitiously watched the teacher.

As the youngsters filed out of the room, Emily stopped Frida outside the door. "Why did you laugh at Mister Jones?" she scolded.

"'Cause he's funny," the girl answered, grinning.

"That's very impolite. You shouldn't make fun of other people's misfortunes. I hope this doesn't happen again."

"I'm sorry, Miss O'Neill. I couldn't help it." She lowered her eyes. "Hope he doesn't come to school anymore," she said softly.

"Why?"

"It's not the same when he's here."

"Don't you like Mister Jones?"

Frida shook her head.

"Why not?"

"'Cause he's too big and fat."

Puddin' Head heard her answer as he walked out the door and he scowled at the child.

Frida saw the look and quickly announced, "Gotta go!"

The big man and teacher stood together watching the young girl run down the path.

"I ain't fat," he stated.

"Don't let her bother you," Emily said. "The words 'big' and 'fat' mean the same thing to children." Then, automatically, she corrected him. "I am not fat."

He gave her a cursory inspection. "No," he said, "you ain't fat neither."

Emily couldn't, for a moment, decide whether to laugh or show indignation. She laughed.

He looked at her, surprised, but he liked her laugh. He laughed too although he didn't know why. All he knew was that he was happy being near the lovely young woman.

The thought occurred to her, why he's fairly attractive when he's not wearing that surly face. She lost her smile after a bit and looked at him seriously. "Mister Jones, I can't have you as a student. It's too disruptive to the rest of the class. I'm sorry."

Puddin' Head was more sorry. He wouldn't be able to see her and spend time with her. He nodded. "Yes ma'am, I'll tell Ma."

She gave him a sad look, then turned and walked away. Her leaving was causing him such distress that, without thinking, he called to her. "Miss O'Neill!" When she turned he experienced a moment of panic, trying frantically to think of something more to say. Then he remembered. "Ah'll come back and fix the floor Saturday."

She smiled. "Thank you, Andrew."

He watched her going down the path to the street and on to Missus Larson's boarding house. A thought occurred to him as he walked behind the schoolhouse to his horse tethered in the meadow and he muttered aloud, "At least I larned one thing in school today—I sure do like that teacher."

# 2

The woman was sitting on a buckboard in front of the schoolhouse when Emily walked out the door the following afternoon. She had obviously been there for some time. The reins were loosened so the horses could graze. The teacher noted a sizable semicircle of grass clipped short and the amount of droppings. Then she did a quick appraisal of her visitor as she acknowledged the good-byes of her students.

Perched rigidly upright on the hard seat, the woman appeared tall and spare. The long, dark print dress she wore almost hid elaborately engraved boots. Her face was shaded by a broad Stetson hat, but as Emily approached the rig, the woman's strong, even features were revealed. A good face, she thought.

"Hello, I'm Emily O'Neill. Were you waiting to see me?"

"Ya," a low-pitched, husky reply. "I be Missus Yones, Karen Yones. Ve talk."

"Oh yes. You're Andrew's mother." She tried to hide her nervousness. "Would you care to come inside? It's cooler."

The Jones woman hesitated for a moment, reluctant to confront the teacher on her home ground. Then, with a slight shrug, she bounded off the buckboard with agility that surprised the younger woman.

She's got to be in her fifties, at least, Emily told herself, and not as tall as I thought. "Will your horses be all right?" she said as they walked toward the school building.

"Dem vil stay." The determined look that Emily saw on the other's face convinced her that the horses would not even think of leaving.

Karen Jones paused inside the door to look around the interior. Her inspection took in the rough tables and benches used by the students. On the opposite end of the room, behind the teacher's chair and larger table, was the oversized blackboard that Emily had requested in her correspondence with the town council. It had been sent all the way from Chicago.

The potbellied stove stood in one corner of the room and a cabinet holding books, slates and other materials, occupied another. There was a map of the world tacked to a wall and a picture of president Cleveland. In the corner to the left of the doorway was a stand that held a wash basin and a large pitcher. On the wall to the right was a row of pegs to hold coats.

Emily cleared her throat. "I can get the chair for you. It's more comfortable than these benches."

The older woman pulled a bench back from the table and sat down. "Det er godt." She pointed at an adjacent bench and indicated that Emily sit. Emily sat.

"Andrew say du don't teach. I pay tax— more dan udders. Du take money but du don't teach."

The teacher wilted under the scathing reprimand. She had to admit to herself that the woman's argument was valid. Anyone who paid the school tax had the right to send a child or a grown man or (for all she knew) a donkey to school. Emily had been made aware of the woman and of the significant contribution she made to the school fund. She was definitely someone the teacher didn't want to offend.

"I...I'm s...sorry, Missus Jones," she stammered. "Having an adult in class as a pupil was disturbing to the other children. They couldn't concentrate on their studies. I didn't know what else I could do." Then her teacher's curiosity took control. "Excuse me, Missus Jones, but why did you want Andrew to attend school this late in his life?"

There was a long pause and Emily wondered if her question had been understood. She squirmed on the bench waiting for an answer. Then she began to worry that she was being too presumptuous. Just as she was about to start issuing more apologies, the woman began to speak.

"Iss hardt to verk big ranch. I haf not much school—litt in old country."

"Is that Sweden?"

She glared at the teacher. "Nei! I be Norsk—Norvegian. I come to America ven I be tventy-one."

"Alone?"

"Nei. I come vit husband...", then seeing Emily's startled look, "...mine first husband, Mister Knudsen." Her face brightened when she spoke his name. "Mister Henrik Knudsen." The young woman wondered at the thoughts of her visitor who sat staring at the wall for a long period without speaking. "Ve live nord of Åndalsnes in lille dalen...I mean little valley. I mix vords ven I tenke Norsk. Mine Engelsk not so good. Boys talk Norsk at hjem. Mr. Yones also talk Norsk litt."

Emily smiled encouragement. "You're doing just fine. But Andrew talks English." Not very well, however, she thought.

"Ya. Mister Yones talk Engelsk to boys at hjem...home. Henrik, mine old son, had school for five year before teacher die. He hjelp Andrew and udder boys litt."

"So Henrik was named after your first husband? What happened to his father?" Emily wanted to hear more about Norway.

"Knudsen farm vas next to Brandrud farm—mine familien farm. Henrik og I play ven små—ve know ve marry ven big. Alvays ve know. I got vit child so ve marry soon. Henrik had no ting—no farm, no verk. Henrik not old son in famlien. He nummer two. Old son get farm in Norge. Henrik say ve go til America—mye lands in America. Ve vil have big farm."

"Is that when you came here?"

"Nei. Ve go til Minnesota. Know Norsk peoples der. Knudsen og Brandrud familien hjelpe—give money. So ve go. I vit child. Much 'fraid. Yust me og Henrik."

The teacher shook her head in sympathy.

"In Minnesota ve take mye...much, I tink, is vord...lands for farm. Norsk peoples hjelp. Verk hardt. Good farm. Much foods. First son come. Den Inyuns come." Misery showed on the face of the older woman. "Kill many hundre peoples. Kill Henrik."

"Oh no!" The cry escaped Emily's lips. "Was this in the New Ulm area?" The young woman remembered hearing of the massacre of Minnesota settlers by the followers of Little Crow in 1862.

"Ya. Seks Inyuns come til huset...house. I holde big gun. Henrik go out—talk to Inyun. Inyun vant ku...cow. Henrik say no. Vi ha bare one cow for milk—milk for babe. Inyun shoot

Henrik. Here." Missus Jones pointed at the center of her chest. "I shoot. Knock one Inyun from horse. Udders run avay."

Emily looked at the older woman with new respect. "Oh my!"

"I hjelp Henrik in house. Henrik hurt bad. I can not stop blood. Vant to go for hjelp. Henrik say no. Inyun vil come back. I hold min husband all natt. He die in morgenen."

Tears were streaming down Emily's cheeks. "That's terrible. They killed him just for a cow. Then you were all alone. What did you do?"

"I bury," she said, reaching over the table and patting the teacher's hand. "One day Mister Yones come. Say many peoples 'fraid—vant to go from Minnesota. Vay from Inyun. Vant to go til Oregon. Good lands in Oregon. Inyuns not kill peoples. Mister Yones say he take mange...many...familie. I say I go. 'Fraid to stay. 'Fraid for lille Henrik. Trade farm for vagon and horse. Ve go in spring, tre-og-sexty."

"In eighteen sixty-three," the younger woman acknowledged.

"Mister Yones vagon-master. Ve go for tolv uke."

"Twelve weeks?" Emily could have bitten her tongue.

"Ya...ya, vat you say...veeks. Ve go tru Dakota and into Montana til ve see stort elven."

The teacher knew the words for "big river".

"Den ve stop." She waited for Emily to ask why. Then continued. "Vun vagon broke. Mister Yones say ve must vait tru vinter. He like land. Vant to stay."

"Didn't the others want to go on?"

"Ya. Mister Yones say he take alt vant to go in spring."

"Why didn't the company continue and leave the broken wagon behind?"

"Nei. Can not do." Emily saw the stern woman actually blush. "Det var min vagon—alt mine tings I can't leave. Mister Yones...,how you say..., had his eye on me."

Emily chuckled. "So it was your wagon. Did the others ever go on to Oregon?"

"Ya. Fem...five...vagon go. Ve marry before he go. Mister Yones komme back in fall. I am vit nummer two son." She patted her stomach.

Emily was amused by the easy manner the woman mixed English and Norwegian words seemingly having no concern whether she was understood or not. If it had not been that during Emily's childhood the O'Neill household had employed a Norwegian cook—a woman who became like part of the family until she left to get married—the teacher would have had greater difficulty carrying on the conversation with her guest. "So that is why the town is called Broken Wagon."

"Ya. Mister Yones say furst big ting here min vagon broked. Det skulle bli name"

With that, Emily threw back her head and laughed.

Missus Jones smiled at the young woman's delight. "Ya. Mister Yones make name for town." Then she laughed with the teacher.

After the last giggle had subsided the two regarded each other with growing affection. "May I get you a cup of water?" The older woman had been fanning herself with her hand.

"Ya takk. Jeg er litt varm."

Emily filled a tin cup from the pitcher. "So you moved here to get away from the Indians? Have they been any trouble in this area?"

"Litt. Inyuns komme some times. Took horses. No peoples killed. Army fight in Sout. Sioux kill mange soldyur of Crook og Custer."

"Oh yes. I remember. About ten or twelve years ago. General Crook fought the Indians just a few days before Colonel Custer's battle on the Little Big Horn."

"Ya. Now I tink all Sioux go out of Montana. Go til Canada. Det var godt!"

"I can sympathize with your feelings, having lost your husband to those savages. Now, at least, you don't have to worry about them. It must be difficult for you having a ranch to look after. Andrew told me that Mister Jones had died. How long ago was that?"

"Tre year. Fall from horse." She tilted her head with her hands and made a cracking sound with her tongue. Emily winced. "Ya. Mister Yones not so good med horse. Big, like Andrew."

Probably clumsy too thought the teacher. "You must miss him terribly."

"Ya. He good man. Verk hard. Good man for boys."

Her lack of emotion told Emily that the woman's true love had been killed by the Indians. "How many sons do you have."

"Henrik Knudsen nummer one, neste kommer Zachary, neste er Franklin, den William and Andrew. Mister Yones name sons for presidents."

Emily chuckled. "Do you have any daughters?"

"Nei, yust boys. Best for ranch. Datter do no ting out der." The wave of her arm took in the whole world outside the schoolhouse.

Emily felt obliged to say something in defense of women but then decided to hold her

15

Irish nature in check, at least for the moment. It was time to approach the real issue at hand. "But if you need your boys for the ranch, why do you want Andrew in school?"

"Andrew og far samme...er...same. Not so good med horse. Meget stor...big. Mister Yones good for make ting...build. Teach Andrew." The older woman paused to look around the schoolroom again. "Andrew built school."

"He did?" The teacher was astonished. "All by himself?"

"Nei. Udder mens hjelp litt. Andrew do most. Verk mange veeks."

Emily was impressed. "Why that's wonderful. He's very accomplished." Missus Jones frowned. "He does very good work," the teacher added, reminding herself that her visitor's vocabulary was limited, although it was obvious she understood more than she could speak.

"Ya. Not good for ranch verk. Not...how you say...?" The older woman fidgeted with her hands trying to form the word. Finally she tapped her skull with one work-worn finger.

Emily picked up the clue. "Are you telling me that Andrew is a little...slow?" The answer was a slight shrug. "Then why not send one of the other boys—Henrik Knudsen, since he's already had some schooling?"

"Henrik go—not here."

"Go? Where did he go?"

"On skip."

"On a ship? Is he a sailor?"

"Ya. Mister Yones dead, Henrik go. Vant to see vorld."

The young woman's face showed sympathy. "So he left, just like that., and when you needed him most." She decided she didn't like Mister

16

Henrik Knudsen Jones very much.

The other shrugged. "Ya. Henrik good med nummer. Know pris for cattle. Go til bank. Do papir vork. Mister Yones not so good med papir."

"So you're hoping Andrew can learn to take care of the ranch business?"

"Ya." Uneasily.

"Missus Jones, that might take a long time. He would have to start in first grade like six and seven year old children. That would be extremely embarrassing for a grown man. Are you sure you want him to do this?"

"Jeg trenger noen i familien som kan skrive regnskapet for meg og de andre guttene skal hjelpe meg med arbeidet." In frustration, the older woman had abandoned English entirely.

Emily shook her head. "Nei! Nei! Du snakker for fort." She was as surprised as the other woman that Norwegian words came out of her mouth.

"Du snakker norsk?"

The teacher shook her head and laughed. "Bare litt. Min familie hadde Norsk kokke." Although she was remembering more and more of the Norwegian that she hadn't heard since childhood, she thought it prudent to retreat to safe territory. "I'm sure you know much more English than I do Norwegian."

The older woman smiled and repeated her earlier statement slowly. "Jeg trenger noen i familien..."

Emily frowned trying to recall the words. "You need someone in the family..."

"...som kan skrive regnskapet for meg..."

"...who can write..." Here she struggled, "...regnskapet? Is that the same as keeping records or books?"

Now it was Missus Jones who showed puzzlement. "Nummer bok."

"Accounts. Of course."

The other woman nodded. "...og de andre guttene..."

"...and the other boys..."

"...skal hjelpe meg med arbeidet."

"...shall help me with the work." Emily giggled with self-satisfaction. "I didn't realize I'd remembered that much. But isn't there anyone else around that can help you with the paperwork—Mister Cotter at the bank, for example?"

"Nei. Jeg ikke like Mister Cotter. Han not Norsk. Skulle bli noen i familien..., ellers du."

"Someone in the family, or me? Why me? You barely know me. Don't you like anyone who isn't Norwegian?" Emily grinned mischievously.

The other smiled back. "Jeg like deg. Kan du hjelpe meg til Andrew ferdig? Jeg vil pay."

The teacher was taken aback by the request. "But Missus Jones, I already have a job. I just wouldn't have time to look after your business affairs and I really don't believe I could teach Andrew in my class so he could ever be ready to take over the bookkeeping."

"Du kan ha ekstra yobb—teach Andrew om kvelden."

"An evening job? I couldn't possibly. I have school work to prepare, papers to grade..."

"Jeg pay sju dollar uke," the older woman interrupted.

Emily was about to continue her argument when the woman's words registered. "Seven dollars a week?" That was almost as much as her teacher's salary. Money wasn't the reason she had accepted the position that was offered in a place with the name of Broken Wagon in the territory of Montana. Quite the contrary, it was more of a lark—a chance to experience the "wild West". But a double in salary was more than she could have ever hoped to receive anywhere else and more than any other graduate of Smith College would be receiving. Besides that, there was the opportunity of witnessing, first hand, a state being born. That was almost certain to happen in the coming year. Now the thought of so much money made her head swim. She could order fine clothes from Chicago or New York, get some perfume and jewelry, start setting some money aside for the future. Of course she would be giving up much of her free time. "I'll have to think about it," she said finally, "and I'll have to talk with Missus Larson about using her parlor in the evening."

"Nei," Missus Jones said firmly. "Jeg snakke med Larson."

Poor Missus Larson, Emily thought. She doesn't have a chance against Missus Jones.

# 3

"Mister Jones! You haven't been listening to a single word I've said!" The young woman was showing her pupil her most stern schoolteacher expression—at least that was her intention.

"Huh?" Puddin' Head, sitting across the table from Emily, tried desperately to recall the words that flowed sweetly from that lovely mouth, tried desperately to draw his attention away from those bright, green eyes that stared at him accusingly from under the sweeping arches of eyebrows, now drawn together to form the slight creases of a frown. At other times he could not stop himself from watching her hands—those delicate, long-fingered hands that moved as she spoke, seemingly dancing with the chorus of her speech.

"Huh?" he repeated.

"Mister Jones," she said again, imploringly. "If you can't pay attention, we may as well quit trying and not waste your mother's money."

"Oh no! Please, Miss O'Neill!" Apprehension showed on the big man's face—apprehension brought about, in a lesser sense, by the thought of facing his mother's wrath, but mostly by the realization that he would not be spending time with a wonderful girl if she stopped tutoring him. "Ah'll try real hard."

Suddenly quiet, she sat studying her pupil with that way of hers that made him uncomfortable. "Ah'll try real hard," she mimicked, almost matching his baritone. "Is that what you believe to be proper English?"

Puddin' Head ducked his head and muttered, "No ma'am, reckon not."

Emily was somewhat ashamed of herself for chiding him so mercilessly but at the same time she was growing increasingly frustrated with his slow progress.

"Mister Jones, people identify themselves by their speech. If you speak like a cowhand, you mark yourself as a cowhand. However, if you use proper English you're accepted as an educated person. One cannot aspire to a higher station in life without the ability to express one's self correctly." Emily suppressed a smile of self-approval for her eloquent statement.

To her dismay she soon learned that it was lost on her student who sat quietly, obviously absorbed in a weighty problem.

"Station?" he said.

The teacher took a deep breath and allowed herself a few moments to reacquire some of her diminishing patience. "Yes, Mister Jones," she began in a level, controlled tone of voice. "Station is that stature that each individual achieves in his life—his social position among his peers, if you will."

Puddin' Head seemed to accept the explanation and Emily started to breathe a sigh of relief which instantly caught in her throat with his next question.

"Stature?"

The young woman experienced a moment of panic when it occurred to her that she might be losing the capacity to communicate. I can't do this, she told herself. I don't care how much money Missus Jones is paying me—I can't teach him if he doesn't understand what I'm saying. I'm going to tell his mother I don't want the job. We've been here several days and I've accomplished nothing. From all appearances, this is a waste of time—his and mine. I need to feel that I'm making progress to have any sense of satisfaction with this job.

As she pondered those concerns, while silently regarding the young man seated across the table from her, he became increasingly agitated. "Hon...honest, ma'am," he stammered, "ah'll try harder."

She felt, then, a wave of sympathy for the pitiful fool, for she had become convinced that he was simply backward and had reached the limit of his ability to be further educated. He's a child in a man's body, she told herself. And yet, she remembered, he had built the schoolhouse— almost by himself. He had learned to build from his father, so Missus Jones had told her. But how much skill does it require to fit logs and boards together? She had to think about that. Could it be, she wondered, that one could have the capacity for learning only certain skills and not others? Maybe his brain was formed in such a manner that it was receptive to only one type of training. He could be brilliant in his ability to perform certain forms of reasoning, but not others. She recalled having heard or read something about people with that impediment. If Mister Jones suffered such a hindrance, she would never be able to teach him reading, writing, or mathematics—not in a thousand years and his mother would have to accept that fact. She must be made to realize that her son was unique in his ability to do certain things, but that he was entirely unsuited to higher learning. After all, it isn't as if he's an idiot, and he's probably quite content doing the things he does best. That thought, she decided, should be explored.

As his tension heightened, Puddin' Head shifted his feet and squirmed on the chair as the young woman regarded him, in her quiet manner from across the table. When she spoke he started so violently that Emily felt the house shake. It almost caused her to lose her composure, but after several deep breaths, she relaxed. "Mister Jones," she repeated, "do you like to build things?"

"Uhhh..." He didn't know how to answer her question. He wanted to say something that would alter her impression of him as a student so that she would continue as his tutor. If he answered in the affirmative she might believe that he preferred building to schooling, which was true except that building did not offer him the opportunity to keep company with this glorious young woman. If he was negative in his reply, she might think him lazy or otherwise unworthy and that the work he performed was done at the insistence of his mother, which was not true. Most often it was he who suggested the projects, whether it be a new shed, additions to the corrals or another wagon. "Uhhh..., well...ah dunno." He tried to stall for time, but she was relentless.

"Mister Jones, do you understand the question?" Poor dumb thing, she thought as the big man slumped on his chair in misery. He's absolutely hopeless. But that settles it—I'm going to talk with his mother. She's a reasonable person so I'm sure she'll see this situation from my point of view, Emily told herself, not entirely convinced. It shouldn't be so bad. She likes me, so what can she say?

He was staring at the table top and he

didn't look up when next she spoke to him. "That's all for today." That's all for all time, she thought. "Would you tell your mother that I would like to have a word with her after church on Sunday? I'll see her in the schoolhouse."

"Ah'll tell 'er." With his eyes still averted and head bowed, Puddin'head picked up his hat and shuffled out the door.

The young teacher's heart went out to him and she almost called him back. No, she decided. It's got to be done—it's for the best, although the thought of confronting the stern, Norwegian woman filled her with anxiety. "She likes me, so what can she say?" Emily repeated aloud.

# 4

"I pay, you teach! Ve haf deal!" That's what Karen Jones yelled at the teacher in a voice that reverberated off the inner walls of the schoolhouse.

It was Sunday afternoon and Emily sat trembling on one of the hard benches while the older woman stood over her, hands on hips and wearing a scowl that would have stopped a buffalo in full charge. The teacher fully expected a clap of thunder to follow the other's pronouncement. "P...please Mis...Missus Jones, I've tried f...for sev...several d...days. He just isn't learning. Some...sometimes I think he doesn't even h...hear me."

"Han vil høre deg! Jeg sier deg—han vil høre på deg!" The continued tirade, that assaulted the terrified teacher, suggested that Jones' youngest son would listen to his teacher if he had to grow elephant-size ears. Although she couldn't be sure, that was the best translation she could make of the Norwegian words which spewed forth from the angry older woman.

"B...but you shouldn't be wasting your mon...money...I'll return the seven dollars you've pa..."

"Nei!" Karen Jones interrupted. "Det er mine money for vaste, vis jeg vil. Du teach! Ve haf deal!" Those last words echoed around the room.

Emily could not remember a worse time in her life, but then her Irish fire ignited. "I will not!"

she screamed. "It is useless!"

The older woman's reply, after a long pause, was spoken in an almost conspiratorial whisper, which seemed even more threatening than her previous yelling. "Du teach, ellers du gå tilbake New York."

"What? The teacher could hardly believe what she was hearing. "You can't send me back to New York! I don't work for you—not any more. I work for the Town Council!"

"Hvis jeg sier du skal tilbake til New York, du må tilbake til New York." As she spoke she waved a finger before the young woman's face.

Then Emily remembered that the Jones woman paid more of her schoolteacher's salary than anyone else. That was told to her at her first meeting with the Town Council.

"I expect that if you don't continue paying into the school fund, the Council will make it up some other way," she told the other. Even as she spoke, she experienced the sinking feeling that it might not be possible. The population in and around Broken Wagon was anything but affluent. From information, that had come to her during her stay, she knew that the Jones family was much more prosperous than others in the area. If Missus Jones withdrew her contribution, it was doubtful the school would survive unless the teacher was willing to accept a big cut in salary. She decided to voice the thought. "I can work for less to keep the school in operation."

"Nei!" A sardonic smile showed on the older woman's face. "Nei! Nei! Nei! Jeg ogsa har skole land."

"You own the school property?" Emily was astounded.

"Ya. Du go, skole go. Swish!" Jones

actually chuckled, flipping her hand as if brushing away the school.

The teacher watched it flying off into the distance. "You would honestly do that?" She could feel her heart break. The school, the children, those were becoming her whole life.

"Ya," the other answered, almost happily. "Jeg vil."

Emily put her head in her hands. Here was a woman who could not be bested. "You don't leave me much choice," she said, near tears.

"Nei, ikke so. Du ha...choice." Jones turned and walked toward the door, where she stopped and regarded the young woman. "Tink om den. Andrew kommer at Larson plass i kveld." Then she left.

Yes, Emily relented. I don't have to think about it. I'll be at Larson's place this evening tutoring Andrew. There's no other way. I'll teach him, she decided angrily, if I have to pound it into his thick skull.

The teacher spent all that afternoon at the schoolhouse blackboard, pondering the education of her oldest and biggest student. By evening she had worked out the beginnings of a program, but it hadn't come easy. He cannot be taught with the same methods used with children, she had convinced herself. Rote learning is effective with youngsters because they simply accept whatever is told them by the teacher, parents or any other older person. At that point in their lives, they don't know enough to question the material presented to them. If they hear something said a number of times, they can say it themselves.

Hardly more than little parrots, repeating what they'd heard. Andrew's major problem did not, necessarily, stem from the lack of knowledge but from not knowing how the knowledge applied to himself. Emily admonished herself for her lack of foresight. He's a grown man, for heaven's sake. Having to sit and practice making letters on a slate would be humiliating for any adult, but he's too shy to complain. He can't learn the same way a child learns. I've got to try a completely different approach with him. I've got to do it backwards. "Backwards", she said experimentally. She pondered the word and slowly the revelation developed in her mind. "Yes!" she yelled. "Yes!" she screamed in the empty schoolroom.

By the time Puddin' Head arrived at Missus Larson's boardinghouse, Emily was beside herself in anticipation of putting her theory into practice. When the big man crept sheepishly into the parlor, he was startled by the appearance of his teacher. She was actually smiling at him, eyes bright and face flushed. She waited until he was seated. "Mister Jones," she announced, "This evening we're going to do nothing but talk."

Puddin' Head barely stifled a groan.

# 5

He saw her the moment they walked into Grange Hall. She was dancing with Fenwick Appleton, circling him back to back in a do-si-do and smiling radiantly.

Puddin' Head scowled and decided that it had been a mistake to come. Watching her enjoy herself with other men was going to be painful. Why should it bother me? he said to himself. She's just the teacher. But, of course, it did.

He was about to turn and leave when Franklin grabbed his arm and said, "Is that her? Say now, she's somethin'. I think I'm goin' to start school."

The youngest continued scowling as the other brothers moved alongside.

"Is that her?" Zachary took note of the scowl. "Well lookee here. I reckon Puddin' Head's gotten hisself a bad case of puppy love." He grinned at his brother's discomfort. "Sure you ain't gittin' more than just some book-larnin' attention?"

Zachary decided he could be carrying it a mite too far when the bigger man turned on him with an icy stare. "Just funnin'," he said quickly holding up both hands, palms outward.

As she finished the dance, Emily was facing the brothers. She smiled in recognition and excused herself from her partner.

"Andrew, I'm pleased you came." She looked at the brothers and then again at her student in expectation.

He cleared his throat. "Miss O'Neill, these here are my brothers. That's William and Zachary—he's oldest 'cept for Henrik, and he ain't here. The other one is Franklin."

Emily extended her hand to each in turn and murmured his name.

Franklin held her hand longer than Puddin' Head felt was necessary and wondered where his brother learned that highfalutin talk when he asked if the lady would honor him with the next dance.

Everyone turned to watch as Ike set down his glass and picked up his fiddle. He nodded to Clarence on the guitar and they started playing.

"Ah'm gonna dance widda teacher." Bull Bjornson staggered into the group and took hold of Emily's arm. She gasped as she turned toward the man who stood no taller than herself but who seemed to have constant width from broad shoulders to the floor. Little about his face could be determined—hidden as it was under a thick covering of red hair and red beard—except for the fleshy nose and bloodshot eyes.

"Sorry, Bull, Franklin said cautiously, "I spoke first."

Caution was called for when dealing with Bull. It was said in the area that he got drunk faster and mean quicker than anyone else around. Also well known was his strength. That squat body with its thick arms and sturdy legs could lift more than any two men. They told of his hoisting Charley Olsen over his head and throwing him over a wagon.

His answer to Franklin was to start pulling the bewildered young woman toward the dance floor.

"Let 'er go," Puddin' Head blurted out.

THE TEACHER AND PUDDIN' HEAD

Bull stopped and turned slowly around. "Did ya heered what he told me?" he said to his two brothers, Ned and Clive, who stood leaning against the building wall wearing whisky-silly grins. "Did ya heered?" Somewhere back in the beard a tooth flashed. "Maybe you'd like to step outside and make that s'gestion?"

Puddin' Head shrugged. "I don't think she's of a mind to dance with you, so if ya wanna come outside and dance with me instead, that's fine." He turned and walked out the door. The three Bjornsons followed.

"So," Franklin said to Emily, "shall we have our dance?"

"What?" She looked at him, unbelieving. "Your brother went to fight those three men and you want to dance?" She scanned the room frantically. "Where did Zachary and William go? They should be out there with your brother if you're not going to help him."

When the altercation began, the two mentioned brothers, with knowing glances at each other, had faded into the crowd.

"He'll be all right," Franklin answered easily. "By the way, where didja larn to be a teacher?"

She gave him a withering glance and started for the door.

"Wait!" he said. "Don't go out there."

She stopped long enough to ask why not.

"It's not worth seein'," he told her. "There's only three of 'em and them Bjornsons, when they're skunk-drunk, can't fight their way out of a straw basket."

She glared at him. "I think you're a coward. You should be out there helping him. What's the matter with you anyway?"

"He don't need my help. Anybody raised with four brothers like us can take care of hisself."

The sounds of heavy body punches, grunts and groans, brought Emily outside with Franklin trailing behind. "Nice ladies aren't supposed to be watchin' this sorta thing," he said as she grimaced at the scene. "Ya' know," he continued conversationally, "Pa was right. He told us boys when we was pickin' on ol' Puddin' Head, that he was gonna git bigger'n any of us and then there'd come a day of reckonin'. Now the three of us can't handle 'im most of the time. Emily squealed as Ned came flying backward to land at their feet.

"How're doin' there, Ned?" Franklin said amicably. Hear you're tryin' to break that three-year old sorrel now?"

Ned shook his head violently until he could focus on Jones' question. "Not too good," he answered seriously. "Ain't nobody can stick 'im. Damn near..., 'scuse me ma'am,...broke m'neck the last time he threw me."

He struggled to his feet. "Better go," he said, heading back into the fray.

Emily stood speechless.

When Clive came staggering toward the two, Franklin caught and steadied the man. "There ya are," he said pushing the somewhat reluctant contestant at his brother's big fist.

Ned arrived again, headfirst, landing in a cloud of dust.

"Ya know, Ned," the Jones man went on as if there had been no interruption, "you ought to use a hackamore to tie up that gelding's head to the saddle horn on Clive's horse so he can't buck. Get 'im used to carryin' ya 'longside 'nother horse."

It took somewhat longer for Ned to assimilate that new knowledge and formulate a response. "I've thought of trying that, Frank, but pa says it breaks their spirit."

"I dunno 'bout that, Ned," the Jones brother continued. "Me and Billy have turned out some purdy good saddle stock that-a-way, an' didn't git our heads busted doin' it."

"Ned!" Bull shouted from the melee. "Git back in here an' help with this ox."

That time Ned needed Franklin's help to come upright. The Jones brother dusted him off and sent him on his way.

"I can't believe this." Emily showed her consternation. "You talk to this man as if he were a friend."

"He is."

"But he's fighting your brother."

"He's Puddin' Head's friend too—we're all friends."

She shook her head slowly, side to side, trying to fathom that revelation. It's a bad dream, she thought. This can't be happening. I left civilization back in New York. Now I'm in the jungle or I've slipped back into primeval times. These creatures are Neanderthals. "So," she said finally, her voice sounding hollow, "you fight with your friends."

"'Course." He was relieved to see that she understood. "Else we wouldn't have nobody to fight with. No strangers 'round here.

"Hey Bull," Franklin shouted as the stocky man hit the ground a few feet away'. "You're holdin' up purdy good. I didn't think ya'd last this long" He noted that Ned and Clive were out of the fight.

Bull glared at the other and lunged to his

33

feet.

"But don't they get hurt?" She still couldn't work it out in her mind.

Franklin shook his head. "Not much. Little sore for a few days but ready' to go again by the next Saturday night."

Emily squealed and jumped backwards to avoid Bull as he crashed down on his back next to her feet. Blood flowed freely from his nose onto his beard. His eyes rolled about in a rather random fashion until, at last, he focused on the Jones brother. He made a heroic effort to get to his feet, then groaned and fell back. "Frank, ol' pal, was a good fight," he frowned trying to recall, "wasn't it?"

"Yup. One of the best."

"Big son-a-bitch, ain't he?"

"Yup. Growed a mite since ya last tangled with 'im."

Bull let loose a groan. "I'm startin' to git a headache. Lets me and you go git us a lil' drink."

Franklin offered his hand and Bull, after wiping the blood from his beard, took it.

They left a dazed schoolteacher, standing outside the hall, looking at the battered victor as he sat on the ground chatting with the two remaining Bjornson brothers.

# 6

As the buckboard approached the ranch buildings, Emily was impressed with the size of the house and the profusion of adjacent structures—barns, sheds and corrals. "Land sakes, Mister Jones!" she said to the driver. "Did your family build all this?"

The young man grinned. "You'd better get used to callin' me Frank or at least Franklin, Miss O'Neill. There are too many Jones fellers 'round here." He slapped the reins on the backs of the team and the horses resumed trotting. It was a moment before he remembered her question. "Nope, not me, anyway. Pa and Puddin' Head did most of the buildin'. I was out herdin' cows with Billy, Zack and Henrik." His jaw muscles tightened. "That was before Henny lit out and left us to handle it by ourselves."

The teacher didn't miss the bitterness that came with his words. "Well if I'm going to use your first name, you'd better call me Emily," she told him. "Your mother seems determined to make me a regular guest."

"She just wants you handy to get the ranch business sorted out," he said with a wink. "More than that—my guess is she wants you in the family so she'll have a full-time secretary. Have you decided which one of us you're going to marry?"

She faced him with a gasp. "What?" Then she burst out laughing at the brash young man. "What makes you think I'd be marrying anyone way out here in the Montana Territory?" She let her gaze sweep the vast openness that surrounded them. It felt, to the young woman, that she was sitting on top of the world. Every direction appeared to be gradually sloping downward toward the distant horizon. "Marriage is not in my plans," she added.

That brought a brief chuckle from the man beside her. "What makes you think your plans are worth more around here than that pile of cow manure," he said pointing. "There's only one person at this ranch whose plans carry any weight. And I ain't that person. Neither is Billy, Zack or Puddin' Head, but I reckon you know that already. Puddin' Head didn't have much to say 'bout goin' to school." The corner of his mouth twisted upward in a wry grin. "From what I hear, you didn't have much to say 'bout your teachin' him."

That brought a frown to Emily's forehead. "I'm afraid you're correct. Why does your mother try to control the lives of everyone around her?"

"Damned if I know," he answered. "She's always ruled the roost, long as I can remember. Pa was kinda easy goin' so he went along with her, even when she was riding roughshod over him." He shook his head. "Only time I ever seen him riled was when we went up against her. Then we'd catch it."

"It must have been a difficult life for you," she said. "Young men tend to be high-spirited by nature. Didn't you resent her domination?"

He looked at the teacher for some time before answering. "If you mean did we get stirred up 'bout it? Yup. I reckon we did, at times, but she was usually right so we didn't make much of a fuss. Besides," he gave her another grin, "Pa kept us real polite."

Emily silently admonished herself for being so inquisitive, but she wanted to know as much about the Jones family as she could in order to be better equipped for dealing with the mother. "Is that the reason Henrik left after your father died—to escape your mother's authority?"

Franklin's bark of laughter startled the young woman. "You go right for the throat, don't you? What else do you want to know about my loco family?"

That caused the teacher to blush. "I'm sorry," she said. "It's none of my business."

"'Course it is," He grinned at the young woman. "You're tied to us, one way or 'nother, whether you like it or not."

Emily frowned and shook her head. "This isn't exactly what I had in mind when I came out from New York. It's rather doubtful I'll be able to accomplish all your mother wants in the time I'll be here."

"You're leavin'?"

"No. Not soon. I'll be here for a couple of years, anyway." She looked around at the prairie again, noting that the grass had turned brown, signaling the approach of winter. "I'll need to find out if I can tolerate your winters. What's it like? Cold I imagine." She shivered involuntarily.

"Cold," he answered with another quick grin. "But you get used to it. Just pile on more clothes. Ain't it cold in New York?"

The teacher resisted an impulse to correct his grammar. "Of course it is. And New York City, being near the ocean, has a wet cold. Not much different in Northhampton, Massachusetts where I attended Smith College. But the temperature rarely gets much below thirty degrees."

"Thirty degrees!" the young man cried, giving his passenger a look of disbelief. "Why thirty degrees is a nice comfortable January day here in Montana. We take off our coats if we're workin'." Skepticism showed on her face. "It's true," he said. "Any warmer than that and we have to take a dip in the river to cool off."

"Of course you would." She gave him a nudge with her elbow. "Must be difficult pushing those ice floes aside."

They laughed together and he decided that she was one special lady.

"So, now you've got Montana figured out, tell me all 'bout New York City?"

She lifted an eyebrow. "Why do you want to know?"

"Just curious. Can't understand how those people can live, packed in so close together."

"If you were born and grew up there, you wouldn't give it a second thought." Another scan of the vast, open terrain that surrounded the young woman, brought forth a sigh. "I'm having difficulty adjusting to a huge expanse of country where there are so few people. I suppose it's just a matter of being accustomed to certain conditions. I'm sure you would feel as much out of place in New York as I do here."

"Reckon so," he admitted. "But that's one of the things Henny wanted to see—a big city. I'll bet he's seen a bunch of 'em by now. Got a letter from him back a spell. Had to get Hans Vik to read it to us. Says he'd been to Hong Kong and Singapore and a place called Shanghai."

"That's in eastern China."

"China, huh?" He turned to look at her, showing a frown. "Henny knew 'bout them places. He was always readin' a book called geog...somethin'."

"Geography," she prompted.

"Yeah. That's it. He was always talkin' 'bout it too. Told us how he wanted to go to this country and that country and see this thing and that thing. Never was much interested. Reckon I did pick up some larnin' hearing ol' Henny carryin' on, but never had much schoolin'. None of the other brothers did, neither. Only him. Ma was purdy set in her mind about him gettin' educated, and look what it got her."

Emily was becoming uncomfortable with the effect the conversation was having on her companion and decided to change the subject. "What was it you wanted to know about New York in the two or three minutes before we reach the ranch?"

"Ain't important," he said gruffly. After a moment, he faced her with a wry grin. "Pardon my bein' so huffy. I get that way thinkin' 'bout Henny. Course it ain't his fault bein' Ma's personal pet. That's just the way it is."

By the time they had arrived at the ranch, Emily was convinced that she had only scratched the surface in gaining any understanding of the Jones family.

# 7

"Your problem is that you're just too old."

Emily's statement caused Puddin' Head a momentary distraction so that the hammer's impact on the nail, held in the big man's left hand, was just enough off-center to be deflected into the thumb joint.

"Dang!" he yelled, dropping the hammer to rub the throbbing joint. "Sorry, Ma'am," he said giving the young woman a sheepish grin. "That's what I get for being so awkward."

"Oh Andrew!" Emily showed her concern for his injury. "It's my fault. I shouldn't be interrupting when you're trying to work. Does it hurt much?"

Puddin' Head put on his best brave-in-the-face-of-adversity expression. "No Ma'am. Ah do this all the time." He looked at the school teacher longer than intended. Dressed, as she was, in the bright gingham dress, her brown curls showing under a flowery bonnet and her tiny feet encased in high, black buttoned shoes, caused the young man's breath to catch in his throat. He couldn't take his eyes off her.

Although she was accustomed to the appreciative looks she received from men, Emily blushed seeing the worship in his eyes. "I'm sorry. I was just thinking out loud about how we should continue with your instruction. You can't be taught in the same manner I use with the younger students at school. There's so much that you already know, just by being older. All we need to do is try to fill in the blanks. That's why we should just have conversations for the time being. However, it may not be appropriate right now. I better go on back to the house. I just wanted to get away from the paperwork for a while." She twisted her pretty mouth into a wry expression. "Your mother has me setting up a record of ranch operations, but the information I've seen so far is rather sketchy."

"No! No!" Despair showed on his face. "Don't go. Ah don't mind you bein' here. Just puttin' together this ol' shed. Why don't you set right down here in the shade?" He grabbed a low, sturdy sawhorse, brushed off the sawdust and set it next to the building. "Got some water here if you're thirsty." He pointed to the canvas water-bag hanging on a nail.

She declined with a shake of her head and, ignoring the offered seat, began walking around the structure. Puddin' Head watched her until she rounded the corner. Shrugging, he picked up the hammer and resumed working.

"What will this shed be used for?" She had made a full circuit of the building and arrived to watch him as he finished nailing the board.

"Same as the others."

A slight frown creased her brow. "Others?"

"Yup. This is number fifteen. Only five or six more to go. Been buildin' 'em for the last three years"

"Land sakes! Why so many?"

Puddin' Head picked up another board and began marking a line for sawing. He'd learned earlier that it was much easier carrying on a conversation with his teacher if he could keep from looking at that lovely face. "We've been losin' stock in bad winters. Zach figgered shelters

41

would save some. Reckon it did winter before last. That was a rough one. Some of the ranchers were hit hard, but we had these sheds. They're built on skids so the teams can drag 'em out on the range."

"Don't the poor cows get cold anyway? I noticed the opening isn't very big, but there would still be a draft. And there's no floor."

The big man allowed himself a chuckle. "The opening is on the side away from the wind. Besides, if we make sure they're well fed, cattle make their own heat. We spend a lotta days haulin' hay out to 'em durin' the worst weather. The reason there's no floor is 'cause a bunch of cattle being inside for awhile would begin to fill up the place with..." He coughed, embarrassed.

"I see," she said quickly.

"This way we can just drag it off to a clean place."

She nodded her understanding. "It's commendable that you take such good care of your cattle—do the other ranchers do this?"

"Nope. Too much work. Lumber is too hard to come by."

"Then how do you manage?" She wasn't ready to let the matter drop.

He finished sawing a board, gave her a shy grin and shifted his stance uncomfortably. "Well, we're a bigger ranch. We can afford a few more things. Got a lil' sawmill run by a steam engine out in the barn. We go up the river where there's some timber. Float it down to a place near the ranch, fish it out and haul it over here. What lumber we don't have use for, we sell or trade."

"Trade for what?"

"Cattle or hay, usually." He began nailing the board on the wall. "We don't put up much hay ourselves. Easier to buy."

He didn't see her smile of understanding as she waited for him to finish. "So that's why your cattle herd is so large. And, of course, all these transactions are recorded?"

The question caught him off guard, and he recognized its implication. "Uh..., maybe not all."

"Maybe not any?"

Puddin' Head blushed and shuffled his feet. "Think you better ask Zach or Ma 'bout that."

Emily was relentless. "Mister Jones, are you telling me you don't know anything about the finances concerning this ranch?"

The big man's face darkened and he turned away, helplessly beginning a search for another board, which was on a stack next to his legs. After a moment, he gathered himself and turned to face the young woman. "Folks in town mostly pay in cash money. Other ranches send over a steer or two to pay for a few hundred board-feet of lumber. Don't think anybody writes anythin' down."

Emily shook her head—unbelieving. "How can anyone run a business this way?" She stood staring at the doleful man in the manner that he recognized so well until, almost in a panic, he escaped back to his work. "I must create some sort of a ledger, but I don't have the information." She talked aloud, but it was to herself. "The only reasonable approach is to begin by taking an inventory of everything and then develop the records from that date foreword. Mister Jones," she said in an authoritative tone that caused him to forget the measurement he had just made. "How long would it take to do a complete and accurate count of the cattle?"

Puddin' Head hesitated for a long moment.

"Uh..., I..."

"Never mind," the teacher interrupted. "I'll ask Zachary."

"Ain't sure Zach knows neither. Stock's scattered all over the range from hell to breakfast." The big man's face suddenly became crimson. "Oh! 'Scuse me, Ma'am."

"Don't concern yourself." Emily laughed. "I'm hearing language that's a lot worse than that since I've been here in Montana. Of course I've never known anyone who's made an accurate measurement of the distance between hell and breakfast. Can you give me a rough estimate?"

Puddin' Head had to laugh at the brash young woman. "'Fraid not, but I 'spect it's a fer piece."

"A fer piece from hell to breakfast," the teacher said. "Now that's a unique expression. I doubt that a good definition exists so that everyone would know the meaning. Perhaps we should supply one. How about five miles, or twenty miles?"

He was enjoying her teasing and he grinned at her. It came to him, as something of a shock, that he was beginning to feel more comfortable around the woman. The Goddess, that had captivated him before, was starting to become a human. Not that she was any less beautiful, nor that he was any less smitten by her, but her appeal to him was changing into appeal that a man would normally have for a woman he found very attractive. That caused Puddin' Head a certain degree of guilt. He was bothered by his part in allowing this ethereal creature to assume the form of simply another person.

Her voice broke into his thoughts. "Do you have any idea when a count of the cattle was last made?"

Thinking brought a frown to the big man's face. "Well...no." He removed his hat and scratched his head. "Seems like we did that once when Henny was looking after things."

"Henny? That's the nickname Franklin used."

Puddin' Head chuckled. "Henrik. Us boys always called him Henny. William is Billy, Franklin is Frank and Zachary is Zack. I'm...," he ducked his head in embarrassment, "...well, you know. Anyway, he wanted to find out how much stock we had, same as you. Pa didn't think it was needed, but Ma sided with Henny. Must've been more'n ten years ago. I was just a kid, but I 'member helpin' with the roundup. I reckon it was mentioned at the time, but I don't recall how many we counted. Might be written down somewhere. Henny's got some papers in his room. 'Course nobody goes in there—Ma keeps his room just like he left it."

Emily's face showed her astonishment. "Don't you consider that somewhat peculiar? He's not dead...just away somewhere. I expect he'll be returning eventually. Certainly the family would have been notified if anything had happened to him."

Puddin' Head shrugged and replaced his hat. "That's the way she wants it. Don't matter much, anyway...'bout the numbers, I mean. Since then, the herd has changed ever' which way from Sunday. Lot bigger. A whole bunch was sold."

The young woman sighed. "I suppose you're right. We'll need to start over again. It's just too bad Henrik left." The teacher stood silent for a moment, wondering if it might be important to learn more about the oldest brother. "Maybe I will sit for a little while," she said, pointing to the sawhorse. Once seated and with her dress adjusted, she turned her attention to her student. "Why do you think it was so important to Henrik to get away?"

Puddin' Head considered the question as he cleared the other sawhorse of boards and sat facing the teacher. "Henny didn't much care for ranchin'. He was smarter than the rest of us, and curiouser."

"More curious," the teacher corrected.

"More curious," he repeated. "He was always readin' books and tellin' the family what he read. Pa would get a little peeved with him, but he didn't say much when Ma was around. She liked hearin' him tell 'bout the books and pushed him real hard to keep larnin' stuff. He must have fifty books in his room that she had sent from back East. Anything he wanted."

Emily nodded. "Franklin mentioned that your mother treated him special."

"Reckon she did." The big man reached down and picked a nail off the ground. He studied the item as if it held particular significance. "Maybe it was 'cause he was her first born and from her first husband who was killed by Injuns back in Minnesota."

"Yes, your mother told me."

"Ma and Henny went through a lot together...the Injuns and then the long haul out here. Gettin' settled and all. He was with her through the bad times. Guess that made her feel closer to him."

"I suppose it would. Did that trouble you?"

"Naw. Not much. Pa treated all us boys the same." He grinned at her. "Sometimes kinda rough. Bothered Frank and Zach more than me. I reckon Pa sorta favored me 'cause we were workin' together a lot."

"Do you miss your father very much?"

"Some, I reckon, but he was a hard man to cuddle up to." He let loose an explosive laugh in response to the expression on her face.

She blushed and then laughed at herself. "I have a feeling that your father was a very strong, self-assured man and that you inherited some good qualities from him. As for intelligence, I don't believe Henrik is any smarter than anyone else...he simply had all the advantages. I intend to prove that."

"With me?" He could see the fire of a zealot shining in her Irish eyes. "How? You goin' to find me a new brain?"

"You have enough brain. I'm going to work with the one you've got while I'm here."

"You're leaving?" Panic showed on his face.

"Eventually, yes. I'll be around for a few years. I don't want to miss the experience of living in a place as it becomes a state. It should be very exciting. I wasn't alive when New York and Massachusetts were brought into the Union. That was a hundred years ago at the time they ratified the Constitution."

"You think this will happen soon?" His lack of enthusiasm was evident to the teacher.

"Could happen by next year. I understand they're considering some legislation in Congress called the Omnibus Statehood Bill. It means to create four new states—Washington, North and South Dakotas and Montana—possibly next year." She frowned at her student. "You don't seem very interested."

Her student took on his defensive posture,

which the teacher recognized immediately. "Don't know much 'bout government or congress."

She laughed to put him at ease, quickly as possible if she was to make her new teaching strategy effective. He had repeatedly demonstrated an inability to assimilate knowledge under stress. "You're not alone. There are times when it seems that politicians intentionally try to make the workings of government so complicated that ordinary citizens have no idea what is going on. I'm sure I don't know."

His grin showed that she had been successful. He began, once more, to engage in the conversation. "Out here in Montana, we're so far away from the Capital that it's a coon's age before we get any news."

She decided to tease him again. "What is the average life span of a raccoon, anyway?"

He laughed. "You know what I mean." Standing, he lifted the water bag off the shed wall and pulled the wooden plug. She indicated a certain degree of distaste as it was offered. "Sorry, Ma'am. I'll get a cup."

"No no!" she objected as he started walking away. "This will be fine." It wasn't, however. As she tilted the bag upward toward her mouth, its contents sloshed into her face and on her dress. She gasped and quickly began brushing water from her clothing.

The big man was mortified. "S...sorry, Ma'am. Should've told you..."

Emily's laugh interrupted his apology. "It's not your fault I'm so clumsy. It's been a while since I drank from one of these things. I ought to know better." She put the bag to her lips and lifted it with greater care. After she had satisfied her thirst, she handed back the bag.

Puddin' Head stared, for a brief moment, at the open mouth of the water bag, thinking about the lips that had touched it most recently. He resisted a strong impulse to place his lips where hers had been. Suddenly flustered, he quickly replaced the stopper and hung the bag on the wall.

"But that's the very reason it should be changed."

Her words failed to register with him. "Uh...Changed?" He tried desperately to recall their conversation before the water bag incident intervened.

She frowned, wondering if she was losing him again. "The government. Wouldn't it be better to have Montana's problems dealt with here by local citizens than by strangers two-thousand miles away?"

He remembered then. "Yup, Ma'am, reckon it would."

"When Montana becomes a state, it will become almost like a separate country." She assumed her lecturing attitude. "That's what we have in the United States—a number of countries that are bound together for mutual advantage and protection. Each of these countries—or states—has its own government. The head man of each state is a governor, instead of a president. States have their own congreses to pass laws and their own judicial branches, to enforce the laws—just like they have back in Washington." Pausing for breath, she realized, then, that he was not absorbing the information being dispensed so liberally. His expression hadn't changed, but she detected a glaze that had formed over his eyes. "Well," she said. "We don't need to go into this right now. We'll be covering it later.   Besides...," she stood and brushed the backside of her dress, "...I'd better go back in the house.   Your mother will be wondering why I've disappeared."

He stood also, holding his hat.   "Sorry you hafta' go," he said wistfully, "but I reckon I better get back to work too or Ma'll skin me alive."

Before turning to walk away, she gave him a brilliant smile that almost caused his knees to buckle.

# 8

Karen Jones shook her head. "Det blir for mange—too many."

They were seated at the long table that occupied one end of the large room. At the opposite end, a stone fireplace stood as the dominant feature of that area and served as the focal point for a semicircle of rough, sturdy sofas and chairs upholstered in cowhide. The heads of several antlered beasts stared down with glassy eyes from the walls around.

A rotund Indian woman, of indeterminate age, entered through a door on the side wall carrying a large iron kettle with a ladle. Steam emanated from the container along with an aroma that suggested the contents could be nothing other than a beef stew. The woman left and returned shortly with several loaves of warm, fresh bread and a dish of butter.

Andrew stood and fetched his mother's plate from where she sat at the head of the table. As his brothers waited impatiently, he filled the plate with stew and placed it carefully in front of the older woman along with one of the bread loaves. The older brother, Zachary, while remaining seated on the left side of his parent, reached and handed her the butter.

At the other end of the table, where she had been assigned, Emily took note of the proceedings and decided that she had witnessed a regular routine in the family. As the youngest, Andrew was expected to serve the mother and probably had done so since childhood. She was also aware that the other brothers avoided referring to the big man as "Puddin' Head" in their mother's presence. They also used the full names of each other. She's in complete control, Emily decided. A classic example of a matriarchy.

After a moment's hesitation, and a quick glance at his mother, the big man also served the teacher. His reward was a "thank you" and another stunning smile which caused him some momentary confusion as to where he had left his chair. His being seated was the signal eagerly awaited by the brothers to help themselves to the food, which they did in a manner just short of chaos.

As they began eating, the conversation was resumed as if there had been no interruption. "Yes, Missus Jones," the young woman responded. "I understand that you have a lot of cattle, but if we're going to begin proper management of the ranch, we've got to have a starting point—an inventory of all assets."

Icy blue Norwegian eyes met the determined Irish green eyes across the length of the table. "Nei. Too many."

"But Andrew told me that you did a count of the cattle before, when Henrik wanted it done." Emily showed her frustration. "Why not do it again?"

"That was more than a dozen years ago," Zachary interjected. "Herd's five times bigger than it was then, and spread out for miles in ever' direction. Couldn't be done."

Watching his adored teacher shrug her shoulders helplessly, Andrew made a rescue attempt. "We could drive the whole herd over to the river where we could use the high bluffs to keep 'em corralled in. I could put in a fence and gate to keep the stock upriver separated from those down river." Feeling the presence of five pairs of eyes bearing on him, the young man stopped talking in confusion.

In the silence that followed, the teacher was the first to speak. "And...?" she urged.

"Well, we could hold one herd off at a distance while we drove the other herd through the gate for a count. After they were turned out on the range, we could bring the other herd through." Andrew looked from one face to another, trying to determine if consideration was being given his suggestion. No one spoke. Continuing to eat, each seemed lost in thought.

Surprisingly, it was William who broke the silence. "Wouldn't be too hard movin' 'em over to the river. Kinda natural for 'em to drift over that-a-way as it is."

"Be easy enough for one or two riders to hold 'em after we get 'em there," Franklin added.

Emily looked at her pupil. "How long would it take to build the fence and gate?"

The big man lifted his eyes to the ceiling as he gave thought to the matter. "Four or five days. Maybe less. There's a narrow place where the bluffs come down close to the river. Not more'n a hundred yards or so. Reckon that'd be the place to put it."

Karen Jones had not contributed to the discussion at all. Throughout the period she sat quietly eating her dinner. Emily tasted the stew again. "This is delicious," she announced. "How does she make it?"

Franklin loosened a bark of laughter. "Maybe you don't want to know. Agnus goes out next to the river and digs up roots and bulbs, then uses shrubs and herbs to flavor the food. We're 'fraid to ask what it is. I guess there's some sage, but I don't know what else. Said she learned it from her ma."

"Well it certainly is good. Agnus?" Emily said, thoughtfully. "That's an unusual name for an Indian."

"Oh, that's not her real name. We can't even say her Injun name. Ma named her Agnus. In the Bible it means lamb. When she came to us she was timid as a lamb. Now she gives us all what for. She was only about sixteen and married to a big buck who was mostly crazy. Beat her all the time. Damn near killed her."

"Franklin!" Karen Jones admonished the son to her right. That was one of the few words she had spoken since the meal began.

"Sorry, Ma," he said, although he didn't appear to be too sorry. "She's a Sioux. Henrik found her hiding in the willows down by the river and brought her home. Ma looked after her until she got her health back. She's part of the family now."

Emily looked at Karen Jones with new respect, remembering that it was Indians— probably Sioux—that killed her beloved Henrik Knudsen. The lifted chin and the slight smile on Missus Jones' face showed that she was aware of the teacher's thoughts.

At that moment Agnus came back into the room and spoke in rapid Norwegian to the older woman, who nodded. Then, with a frank, curious look at the family's guest, she swept out of the room. She reappeared shortly with two pies.

"Apple," Franklin said. "We have a small orchard on the other side of the barn and Agnus has a real way with pies. So saying, he reached behind and swatted the big woman on her broad backside as she passed behind his chair. She didn't appear to notice as she placed the pies on the table. But, upon departing, dealt the errant young man a pop to the side of the head that nearly knocked him from his chair. He shook his head, laughing. "One of these days she's going to kill me—probably scalp me too."

"Franklin!" his mother said. "Du må være snill!"

Emily was astonished. She'd never known anyone to behave in the manner she had just witnessed. Adding to her confusion was the look of affection that appeared briefly on the mother's face as she regarded her number three son. Why he's a scamp and she loves him for it, the young woman decided.

The others at the table took no notice. "Well, what do you think, Ma?" Zachary paused momentarily from shoving pie into his face to pose the question. "Are we goin' to give the teacher her count?"

Blue eyes and green eyes locked again in quiet combat. Emily took a deep breath. "I don't see how I can be of any benefit at all to you unless this is done."

A long silence followed. The older woman sighed. "Ve må ha hjelp."

"We might get some of the boys from school to help, if their pa's can spare 'em," Zachary said. "They're always ready to pick up a few bucks."

"We've got enough materials," Puddin' Head put in. "I can start tomorrow on the fence and gate."

William wasn't to be left out. "Best I get started bringing them in from way out on the east side. That'll take the longest. I'll ride on over and see if Hans Vik can lend a hand."

Flushed with victory, Emily was barely able to suppress a grin of satisfaction. "How long will it take to bring all the cattle over to the river?"

The brothers looked at each other. "Close to a week," Franklin offered.

"Ten days," Zachary said. "William?"

The most reserved brother of the family nodded. "Yup, all of that, if it's just me and Hans."

"Don't think you'll get any other help." The older brother scratched the whisker stubble on his chin. "We'll be spread pretty thin. Lot of range to cover."

"Well, in that case I won't be needed around here until after the count is completed," Emily said smiling brightly. "I'll go back to town in the morning."

The smile faded abruptly with the sudden sound of Karen Jones' voice. "Nei! nei! nei!" She pointed a finger at the young school teacher. "Du stay! Du count!"

"But...," Emily began protesting.

Her argument was lost, however, in the rising tide of the older woman's words. "Du vant count, du count." That was followed by stream of invective Norwegian oratory that was totally lost on the person toward whom it was directed.

Watching the young woman wilt under the onslaught of their mother's overwhelming demonstration of authority, caused the brothers to exchange grins, except for the youngest. He flushed with embarrassment.

After the room quieted, Franklin spoke. "Ma says you speak some Norse, but I doubt you caught all that. I'll give it to you in a nutshell. From what I understand, you agreed to help

Puddin...," he glanced sheepishly at his mother, "...Andrew with his schoolin' and at the same time set up the ranch like a business with paperwork and all. She says you come out here with your big ideas about how this should be done and now you don't want to be part of it even though you're taking her money. She said some other things that weren't very flattering, but I won't go into that." He gave Emily a devilish grin.

The contrite teacher sat with head bowed, realizing that there was more than a grain of truth in his words. Reluctantly she admitted to herself that she wanted the extra money, but not the responsibility that went along with it. "I'm sorry, Missus Jones," she said in a small voice. "You're absolutely correct. That was very selfish of me. Of course I'll do everything I can to help." She glanced around the table at the brothers. "As soon as the cattle are rounded up, I'll come out to the gate and make a count."

"Nei! Nei! Nei!

Startled, Emily looked at the older woman and saw the same satanic grin on her face as she'd noted on the face of her number three son. "I don't understand," she blurted out.

"Du hjelp med roundup. Du ride."

"Oh I couldn't possibly," the teacher protested. "There's the school."

"Ma can call a two-week recess." Franklin grinned at the young woman and then at his mother. "She can do that since she's head of the school board."

Emily felt she was being boxed in. "But I'm not a horsewoman."

"You've never been on a horse?" Zachary looked at her unbelieving.

"Of course I have." She scowled at the

brother. "I rode some. Mostly when I was a young girl, but I haven't ridden in years."

"Reckon you was ridin' on one of them sidesaddles that the fancy ladies use?" Franklin and his brothers exchanged knowing glances.

"Well...yes, but..."

"Not much good out here for the kind of ridin' we do. A cuttin' horse makes a quick turn and you'll find yourself ridin' air." The other brothers joined in laughter at their sibling's remark.

"But with a skirt...I couldn't..." Emily was feeling uncomfortable with the direction the conversation was taking.

"Skirt hell!" Franklin, in good spirit, took the swat his mother delivered. "Sorry Ma. I just wanted to tell the teacher that you can't ride a western saddle wearing a long skirt." He turned his attention to the young woman. "You gotta do what Ma does when she rides. Puts on a pair of britches and a work shirt. With her Stetson hat and cowboy boots you can't tell her from the rest of us." The grin he gave his mother showed the pride he felt. "And she rides just as hard."

Emily blanched at the thought of putting on men's clothes and riding straddled on a horse. Yet, the idea was intriguing.

"Ma's got plenty of extra clothes," the brother went on. "You're about the same size so there shouldn't be a problem with getting you all decked out."

The young school teacher sat with wide eyes staring at the pictures that formed in her mind. Suddenly, to the surprise of the others seated at the table, a smile spread on her face and she laughed aloud. "Why not?" she said. "Why not?"

# 9

Andrew was standing by the saddled horse when the young woman emerged from the house. He almost failed to recognize his teacher as she approached. In the morning sunlight, the broad-brimmed cowboy hat hid most of her face. While the clothes she wore were masculine in style and cut, the figure contained within was definitely female. The big man could only stand and gape as she approached.

"Well?" she said, showing her embarrassment.

"You're beautiful." He hadn't meant to say that. It just came out along with the blushing. "I...I...mean you look just fine."

She giggled, self-consciously, and then asked about the horse.

"Billy gentled this mare for Ma, but she doesn't ride 'er much. She likes somethin' bigger and stronger with more spirit." Standing alongside, he caused the mare to appear even smaller. "Billy has a way with horses. He took a lot of time trainin' this one. She isn't as big and fast as most of the others, but she'll do anything you want and she isn't skittish."

Emily seemed uncertain. "I've never ridden on a horse straddled. Is it difficult?"

The big man chuckled. "I ain't never ridden sidesaddle. Is that difficult?"

She laughed. "I wouldn't imagine you had. You've probably never worn a long skirt either." She laughed again at his discomfort. "You've seen those saddles, of course, and know they're made differently for women. It's just a matter of what you get used to."

"Well," he said, slapping the saddle with a big hand, "this is what we're used to. I can't say I've ever seen a sidesaddle—heard 'bout 'em—but I did see one of them English saddles that the gentlemen back east use. They wouldn't be no good, neither, for the sort of work we do. No horn, for one thing."

Emily looked at the leather-wrapped knob on the front of the saddle and said, "Is that what I use to keep my balance?"

The Jones brother chuckled. "No real cowboy would ever want to be seen holdin' on to the horn, but I won't tell if you grab hold to keep from fallin'. Mostly it's used to hold a canteen or for somethin' to wrap the lariat around when you're doin' some ropin'."

"I won't be trying to catch any cows," she said, smiling at the man, "so I'll probably be clutching it with both hands." She moved tentatively closer to the horse. "She won't kick me, will she?"

He shook his head, grinning. "Shucks no. This is Ma's pet. She's gentle as a lamb. Let me show you." The big man got down on hands and knees and crawled under the mare. Then he used her back leg and tail to pull himself upright. The horse didn't flinch a muscle. "Don't worry. She'll never hurt you. Give her an apple or a taste of somethin' sweet and you've got a friend for life."

Emily walked around to the mare's head and began stroking the animal below the ears. The mare put her nose against the woman's chest and whinnied softly. "Oh, I love her!" the teacher cried. "What's her name?"

"Ma named her Marta after her favorite girlfriend back in Norway. Said Marta was a calm and very kind person." He smiled at the young woman. "This Marta is like the other one." Andrew didn't bother telling his teacher that the mare was smelling his mother's familiar clothes.

Emily's face became serious. "Are you sure your mother doesn't mind my riding her pet?"

"It's what she wanted. It's her way of makin' sure you're looked after the best way possible." The look he gave her was equally serious. "She really does like you. I can tell you that."

Emily laughed. "Sometimes I wonder."

He removed his hat and wiped his forehead with a sleeve. "Don't let her bother you," he said after a moment's hesitation. "She's kinda rough on everbuddy."

"Everybody," she corrected.

"Everybody," he repeated obediently.

She laughed. "I'm sorry. I just can't stop being a teacher."

"No! It's all right. I want to larn...I mean learn. Everybody! Everybody! Everybody!" he said in a loud voice.

"Stop that!" she said and playfully slapped him on the chest. "Now are you going to teach me how to ride Marta or stand here talking all day?"

The big man was wishing he could feel, for the rest of his life, her hand on his chest, but then he gathered himself enough to focus on her question. He looked at the saddle. "I think the stirrups are about right. They should be set so that you can just stand with your...er...with your...with the rest of you off the saddle." He blushed furiously.

She laughed with that good, hardy, throaty laugh that he loved to hear. "Are you referring to my backside, by any chance," she said teasingly. "In France it's the derriere."

His face and neck were dark red under the tan. "Well...er...well," but then he was laughing with her.

"All right," he said at last. "Let's get to it. Couple of things you should know about cow ponies—the way they're trained. If you leave the reins on the ground, like they are now, the horse will stay put—some longer than others. I think Marta would stand here all day."

"So that's all I need to do if I get off and leave the horse—just drop the reins on the ground?" She frowned. "Why are they trained that way?"

He waved an arm in the direction of the open countryside. "When you're out there on the prairie and you need to leave your horse, there's usually nothin' to tie to, except grass. And that's not goin' to hold nothin' ...er ...er ...anything." He picked up the reins and flipped one over each side of the horse's neck. "Ready to get on?"

"What do I do?" She stepped around him to stand on Marta's side.

He looked at her closely. "From what I've heard, nearly all sidesaddles are made so the lady's legs are on the horses left side, so you mount from the left side. Same thing is true with a saddle like this—mount from the horse's left side. That's what the horse's expectin'. Horses ain't too smart, so if you try to get on from the other side, like Injuns do, they get mixed-up." He gave her a grin. "And you don't want to ride no mixed-up horse."

She grimaced hearing his unrefined

language, but didn't say anything. I'll get to that later, she decided, not wanting to interrupt his instruction.

"On other horses, you'd want to hold both reins, along with the horn, with your left hand. That's to keep the horse steady while you're climbin' on. You won't need to do that with Marta—she won't move until you're ready to go. Now put your left foot in the stirrup...," he noticed she was wearing a pair of his mother's saddle boots, "...and grab the back of the saddle with your right hand. Pull yourself up with both hands."

Marta was not a big horse, so Emily found she could get her foot in the stirrup without much difficulty. Pulling herself up and throwing her free leg over the back of the saddle required a little more effort. When she was seated, she wiggled her buttocks. It's quite comfortable, she thought.

He looked at her with open admiration. "You did just fine. Now hold both reins in your left hand. That leaves your right hand free to swing a whip or a rope." He had noticed, among all other features about her, that she was right handed.

She glared at him. "I'm not going to be whipping or roping any cattle," she said emphatically.

He chuckled. "You don't need to. When you're herdin' cattle, all you need to do is swing the whip or rope around. They get the idea. They've all been caught with a rope before."

"When would that have been," she wanted to know.

"During brandin'," he said in a matter-of-fact manner. "I think they remember that experience very well."

She looked horrified. "Why do anything so cruel as brand a cow?"

He shrugged. "Nobuddy has thought of a better way. We've got to know which cows are ours and which ain't."

The plaintive expression her face assumed, showed that she understood, even though she didn't approve. "I suppose so," she sighed. "What do I do now? Shouldn't I be holding a rein in each hand?"

He shook his head. "That's how you drive a horse pullin' a buggy or a wagon. Maybe that's what you do with the horses you been ridin', but with these saddle horses you pull both reins together to one side or the other. When Marta feels a rein pushin' on one side of her neck, she'll turn the other way. To stop the horse, say 'whoa' and pull on the reins. 'Course you know that, but be gentle on the reins. She'll know what you want to do." He paused until she nodded.

"To get started, just ease the reins and nudge her with your knees." He made a clicking sound with his tongue and the mare started walking. "Just ride around the yard for a while. Turn her, stop her, start her again until you two get used to each other." When the teacher—now the pupil—looked at him with some apprehension, he smiled encouragement. "Later I'll get my horse and we'll take a ride. Ma wants us to work together so we can keep on with my education while we're herdin' cattle. You'll be gettin' a lot of my company."

# 10

Puddin' Head pulled his roan gelding to a stop on top of a rise, hung his lariat on the saddle horn and put a loose knot in the horse's reins. With his hands free, he flexed his arm and shoulder muscles to relieve the strain.

"Whoa, Dagger," he said as the big horse shifted its position. "Steady, now."

After scanning the open prairie, he turned to watch Emily working a herd of a couple hundred head in the flat below. He smiled, recalling the times spent recently in her company. They'd provided entertainment for each other, telling of their past lives. Laughter came forth frequently with the recounting of one ridiculous occurrence or another.

In the past week she'd made good progress toward becoming an accomplished drover. During the four days needed to build a gate and put up a high fence, she'd stayed with the big man, providing help when necessary but, otherwise, practicing her riding. After the first few days, when she'd been so stiff and sore she could barely rise in the morning, she gained confidence and experience rapidly.

The roundup had begun the morning after the decision was made. The crew consisted of family members and two boys from Emily's class, fifteen year old Hans Vik and eleven year old Tom Gardner. No other help had been available. The range had been divided into four general areas with two riders assigned to each. William

65

collected Hans at the Vik ranch and set off for the remote eastern sector. Zachary took young Gardner under his wing to cover the region nearest town so the lad could be at home most nights. Karen and her son, Franklin, worked the range that surrounded the ranch buildings, while a smaller tract in the west, nearer the river, was to be taken over by Andrew and his teacher after the fence and gate had been installed.

Emily could hardly wait to get started. In spite of two falls, which almost caused the big man's heart to stop, he never saw any lack of enthusiasm in the young woman. She was having the time of her life.

He'd tried to warn her of the hazards she faced: "Just remember one thing," he told her their first day on the drive. "Marta is a cuttin' horse. She knows a lot more about herdin' cattle than you. That's what she's been trained to do. If one of the stock tries to get past her, she'll turn to head it off. As it dodges, she'll be jumpin' back and forth to stay in front of it. She'll be doin' this quicker than you can think, so you have to be ready and keep your balance on her while she's hoppin' around. Otherwise you'll be partin' company. She's got her job to do so she won't have time to be worryin' about you. You have to take care of yourself."

Looking into the serious green eyes that regarded him, he was suddenly concerned that she might be so frightened by his warning as to become tentative in her riding. That could prove even more dangerous. To put her at ease, he'd smiled and added, "You'll soon get used to her ways and know what she's goin' to do. 'Til then, just grab hold of the horn and hang on."

Her first fall occurred exactly in the manner

he'd described. The mare had turned abruptly to stop a steer trying to break loose from the herd. Emily fell. Seeing that one foot was caught in the stirrup, Andrew had raced to her rescue. That hadn't been necessary. Marta had stopped in her tracks. The young woman was able to pull her foot out of the boot and was hobbling around when her hero arrived.

"I wasn't paying attention," she'd admitted sheepishly. Taking the boot from the stirrup and putting it on, she dusted herself off, climbed back into the saddle and continued the drive as if nothing of any significance had occurred.

From the rise, Puddin' Head looked around again. Satisfying himself that no strays were in view, he turned again to watch the woman he adored. His breath caught in his throat. A steer had broken away from the herd and was racing back in the opposite direction. He saw Emily turn the mare and start after the steer. In spite of his fear, the big man knew he had never seen anything so marvelous. The mare was stretched out in a full gallop with her rider leaning foreword so her face was almost buried in the flying mane. Marta was not a fast horse so the race continued for some time.

Please be careful with her, the big man implored the mare from a distance. It had been during just such a hard ride that Emily had suffered her second fall when the horse stumbled in soft earth. After some tears and assurances that nothing was broken, the plucky woman had resumed riding.

The experience appeared to have had no lasting effect on her—she still rode with the same reckless abandon as before. Andrew was able to breathe freely again when he saw the mare gain the lead on the steer and block its retreat. He watched as Marta did a dance with the steer—her rider swinging the rope and flowing with every move—until the wayward animal gave up and turned back toward the herd. He couldn't see her face from his location, but knew it was shining with excitement. His pride knew no bounds.

On the drive they talked endlessly. When the cattle were moving along without resistance, they drifted together behind the herd and resumed their conversation. The teacher used those opportunities to acquaint her pupil with subjects that could be presented by discussion such as language, history and government. As familiarity grew, he lost all reluctance in asking questions and she soon learned, much to her surprise, that she had misjudged him completely. He demonstrated a high degree of intelligence and an inquiring mind. Emily was hard pressed, at times, to provide satisfactory answers to some of his queries, saying, "That's something we'll have to look up when we return to the ranch."

Their nights were spent on the prairie. It wasn't practical to ride to the ranch in the evening and return in the morning, although he tried to encourage her to do so. "You can't get a good night's sleep here on the ground. I'll look after the herd myself."

She had declined, emphatically. "I can stay out here just as well as you."

Nevertheless the big man was deprived of some sleep in the night, rousing frequently to maintain the fire so the woman in his care wouldn't be too uncomfortable. Several times he awoke to find her snuggled close, unconsciously seeking warmth. Although it was delightful to feel her near to him, he always carefully eased away, fearing she would waken and suffer embarrassment.

Packed in her saddle bags were books, slate and chalk, so the two spent their evenings sitting close together, next to the fire, while she gave instruction to her student. The youngest Jones looked forword to those sessions with high anticipation. Remembering her warm presence against his shoulder, he could hardly think of anything else during the day.

Two wagons were dispatched from the ranch each afternoon to track down the riders and provide them with needed supplies, including firewood and prepared dinners. One was driven by Agnus—the other by her son, Hagen, the product of an unholy alliance between the Indian woman and an itinerant saddle tramp some sixteen years previous. Otherwise the riders subsisted on cold tack carried in saddle bags.

On a number of occasions they found cattle from the adjoining ranch mingling with those branded JK. When Emily first noticed the Jones' brand—the two letters joined with a common vertical segment—she mentioned to her companion that it was thoughtful of his father to name the ranch after his wife, Karen.

"I suppose you could look at it that way," he said chuckling, "but his name was Kent, so he had them both covered."

"I didn't know that," she said. "Your mother always referred to him as Mister Jones."

"She did all the time they were married. Never called him Kent." A quick grin showed. "To us boys, he was Pa. I didn't know for a long time that he had a first name."

When they saw the strays, she asked about the V brand.

"Those are from the Bar V ranch—Alf Vik's spread, he told her. "We'll cut 'em out and send 'em south toward his place. Any of ours, gettin' down on his spread, always come back."

"Has Mister Vik ever sold or traded any cattle to the Jones ranch?" She wanted to know.

Andrew frowned, thinking. "Some, I reckon. Most of the other ranches have too, at one time or another." Then he smiled, knowing what her next question would be, so he provided it for her. "How do we know some of these strays aren't ours? Usually we try, one way or another, to get rid of the one's we've bought or got in trade. Some we sell. If we need meat, we'll slaughter a couple. We rarely get a heifer—folks hang on to their breedin' stock. If we do, we just add our brand next to the old one." He gestured toward the strays. "None of these are ours."

Still Emily wasn't satisfied. "As I understand, when the cattle go through the gate to be counted, and some are found without brands, they'll be branded at that time."

"...And fixed," he said without thinking.

"Fixed?" She looked at him shortly.

His neck and ears showed sudden color and he avoided her eyes. "...Aaah...fixed. You know? The bulls."

It was her turn to blush as she caught his meaning. "Oh. I see." Then she laughed at the two of them. "Can't we just say the word 'castrate'?"

He laughed with her. "I reckon we can."

As her laughter died, it was replaced with a frown. A question came to mind and she put it into words. "How come you always castrate young bulls? If I remember anything about biology, I'm quite sure you need bulls along with cows to produce calves."

"Yes," he said with a grin, "but they don't have to be married. These longhorns don't make very good wives anyway. Too ornery. As it is, one bull can take care of the needs of fifty or a hundred cows. And we have very select bulls— Herefords. That's a breed of cattle that comes from England. There's one." Andrew pointed to a stocky red animal with a white face. "There's another over there. We have twelve all together.

"The folks heard 'bout a feller named Charles Goodnight down in Texas. He started crossin' his longhorns with Herefords about ten years ago. The offspring have more meat of better quality. Pa and Ma thought that was a purdy good idea, so they started buyin' Hereford bulls from back east. Cost several hundred dollars each with the shippin'. They got rid of the longhorn bulls, so now all we have is the Herefords. We're tryin' to breed outta the longhorn business."

Her nod indicated acceptance. "Why did your folks get into the ranching business in the first place?" Emily was curious and he seemed to enjoy talking about it.

"Some fellers were drivin' longhorns up here from Texas to sell to miners. Pa could see the land wasn't much good for farmin', but thought it might be fine for raisin' cattle. He had some money saved from takin' wagon trains out west, so he bought a bunch of heifers and a couple of bulls. So did some of the other settlers here." He grinned at his teacher, who was now the student. "That's the way it started. Look at it now."

"All these cattle," she marveled, then continued to press the earlier issue, "Are you sure those without brands are yours?"

"We don't know for certain. On a ranch this size, it's easy to miss some stock. We try to get over the whole spread as often as we can but, since Henny left, it makes that much more work for everbuddy...er...everyone else."

She smiled with the satisfaction of knowing she was making some progress in his education. His speech was improving to a small degree. "Then sometimes you claim cattle that might not be yours?"

"Yup." His look was one of chagrin. "All the ranches do it. We try to keep the stock separated, but it's not always possible."

"Doesn't this sometimes create controversy between neighbors?"

He frowned. "Contro...?"

"Disagreement. Quarrels." She reminded herself that his vocabulary was still limited.

"Not much. We try to get along." Andrew smiled into those Irish eyes. "So far no range wars."

Still, the teacher was having difficulty accepting such an easy-going attitude in conducting business. It did not fit with her idea of organization, but she decided to let the matter drop...for now. There would be time to do something about that later.

# 11

What would my parents think of their college-graduate daughter now, Emily asked herself. She was coated with dust kicked up by the herd she was following. Only twice had she been able to get clean since she and Andrew (she winced every-time she heard the name, "Puddin' Head") had begun their part of the roundup. The first opportunity occurred when the herd had stopped at a creek. She'd slipped away to an area upstream of the cattle, hidden by trees and bushes. There she stripped and washed herself in the cold water and changed into the extra shirt, stockings and boy's underwear she'd brought along.

Before donning her denim trousers, a violent shaking had been needed to reduce the accumulation of dust. She'd tried to pull a comb through her curls, but it was too much trouble. Instead, she'd settled for piling her hair on top of her head and covering it with her hat as she'd done since the drive started.

Andrew had perceived the purpose of her absence and had, thoughtfully, provided a fire. This was gratefully appreciated by the shivering young woman upon her return.

Two days later they'd passed a point which would mark their closest proximity to the ranch. It was here the big man had insisted she take the rest of the day off for an overnight stay at the house. She'd been too tired to offer much resistance.

Upon arrival, filthy and bedraggled, she'd been met by Karen Jones who'd smiled her approval. "Ya, godt," she'd said. The older woman had been preparing for departure but lingered until she was sure Emily had a warm bath and a hot meal prepared. Afterwards, the teacher had fallen into bed and slept twelve hours straight.

On the sixth day of the drive they reached the river and turned the cattle downstream. Soon they came to the area where the buttes confined the herd so it was forced to travel alongside the river. That greatly simplified the drovers' work, and the two were able to ride together.

"Gate's only about three miles ahead," he told her.

"Do you think Zachary's herd is in front of us?"

"Probably," he answered. "He had farther to go, but then he had four days head start. There's a break in the buttes up yonder where he'll bring his herd through. We'll be able to spot the tracks if they've been there."

Emily smiled at her companion. "So we'll start the count in the morning?"

"Yup," he said. "You'll be sittin' up there on that little platform for quite a spell." He had put together an six-foot tall stand for seating two people where they could look down on the stock from their position at the side of the gate.

"Your mother's and William's herd will be held about a mile downstream?" She wanted assurance.

"Just like we decided." The big man paused to wipe his face with a big red neckerchief. "After they go through the gate, we can turn these cattle out onto the range without gettin' 'em mixed with their herd."

She nodded. "It will be good to get it over with." She laughed at the big grin he showed her. "Don't say it! Don't remind me that the whole thing was my idea. I don't want to hear it."

"Didn't say a thing." Andrew matched her laugh, then pointed ahead to where the river had formed a bank of ten or twelve feet high. The herd divided with some of the cattle trailing single-file under the bank adjacent to a heavy growth of willows and cattails that grew along the river. "You go down and follow those so they don't turn back. I'll keep the rest movin' along up here."

She followed the last of the stragglers down below the bank. The cattle kept to the narrow path—none seemed interested in trying to bolt through the brush. That made her task easy. Too easy. She was nodding in the saddle when he leaped out from the his hiding place in the willows and grabbed the reins of the mare. She screamed when he pulled her roughly from the saddle and climbed on the horse. She saw, then, that he was an Indian and knew he wanted Marta. The ends of the reins were still in her hands and she hung on with grim determination. As he fought her for the reins, the terrified animal kept backing away, dragging the woman.

Then she saw him pull out a knife. "No!" she screamed. "No!

At that moment, a huge form emerged from the bank above and fell on the mounted Indian with a startling impact that carried the three rolling out into the willows and bulrushes. Emily had lost her grip on the reins but, after much thrashing around, the mare reappeared and allowed herself to be caught by the woman.

Then Andrew walked out of the brush dragging the Indian by the hair. "Are you hurt?" His face registered concern. "Did he hurt you?"

"N...No," she said. "I'm all right."

"Your face," he said, looking closely, "it's scratched." He seemed to have forgotten the Indian he was still holding by the hair.

She put her hand to her cheek and studied the trace of blood on her fingers. "It's nothing. Why he's just a boy," she said when she could see the Indian clearly for the first time.

He turned to look and gave the youth careful scrutiny. "Reckon about fifteen or sixteen. Can't tell what tribe he's from. Most of the Sioux have cleared out for Idaho or Canada, but there's some other tribes around. Could be Shoshone, but they usually don't get out this way." He grinned at the girl. "Reckon this young buck figgered to be a big man around the lodge tonight if he could steal a horse."

"What's that he's doing?" The youth, still hanging by his hair with his knees on the ground, had his eyes closed and was chanting rhythmically.

The big man listened for a moment. "I don't understand the lingo, but I reckon he's singin' his death song. Thinks I'm gonna kill 'im."

"Y...You're not,...are...are you?" she said, wide-eyed.

"Shucks no!" He shook his head, grinning. "Then I'd have to contend with Agnus gettin' all over me for doin' in one of her people. But I am goin' to do this..." With that, he lifted the youth to his feet, spun him around and planted a big boot onto his behind with a force that sent the Indian sprawling in the dust. When the young man looked around, he saw the glaring giant pointing upriver with an emphasis that could not be misinterpreted. The youth showed quick comprehension, for he was on his feet in an instant, running headlong back along the path that Emily had recently traveled.

The young woman watched the retreating figure. "He won't come back, will he? He frightened me out of my wits."

"I doubt he'll stop runnin' before he hits Wyoming."

"Do you think there's any more in there." She looked fearfully into the willows alongside the trail.

Andrew saw the worry on her face. "Ride back to where you can get on top. If the herd has started backtrackin', head 'em off and bring 'em along." He pulled out his revolver and handed it to her. "Nobody is going to bother you if they see you have a gun. If you have to use it, just pull back the hammer here..." he showed her, "...and shoot in the air. That should scare off anybody." She seemed hesitant. Then he showed her the familiar grin. "It won't bite...only if you want it to."

"He had a knife." Emily shuddered involuntarily.

"You're lucky he didn't have a gun." He began searching through the willows. "Even the young ones can sometimes get hold of a gun. Reckon Custer's cavalry left them a purdy good supply of weapons down there on the Little Big Horn. Yup! Here it is." He emerged from the brush carrying the blade, which he studied for a moment. "Not an Army issue. Probably got it in a trade."

He put the knife in the mare's saddlebag and then stooped to pick up her lariat that had been dropped. After he had coiled and hung it on her saddle horn, he remembered. "Oh, and catch my horse while you're at it. I'll follow this bunch till they can join the others."

"On foot?"

"Won't be far. I'm more used to walkin' than ridin'." He held the mare while she mounted. "If you see any more Indians, just give 'em your schoolteacher look. That'll send 'em skedaddlin'."

"Oh you!" She gave him a look of feigned annoyance, and then smiled.

He chuckled watching her ride off with the pistol held in plain view.

They were riding together again when Andrew pointed and said, "There they are."

At a break in the buttes, she saw a wagon with several people milling around. "Must be Zachary and Tom," she said, squinting, "but who are the others?"

"Probably Ma and Frank," the younger Jones replied. "That's Hagen's wagon. It doesn't have a cover. Ma probably left Agnus, with her wagon, downstream to hold the other herd."

As they approached, she saw that he was correct. The boy, Tom, came riding down the slope to meet them. "Howdy, Miss O'Neill," he greeted his teacher with a shy smile. He could hardly believe she was the same woman he knew in the classroom. "Mister Jones." He nodded cautiously to the big man. "Missus Jones said for you to come and get fed. I'll take the herd up to the gate with the rest of 'em."

The teacher returned the smile. "Why

thank you, Tom. That's very nice of you."

Zachary was the first to speak when they reached the wagon. "Finally got here, huh? We came in yesterday. Ma and Frank had their herd at the river before that. So did Billy and Hans. What kept you?" he said to his brother.

"Slow cows." Andrew stepped down from the saddle and playfully pulled his older brother's hat down over his eyes. He gave Franklin a light punch on the chest as he walked past toward his mother. There he removed his hat so he could give her a brief hug and a peck on the cheek. "You must've been hustling that herd somethin' fierce," he told her.

She patted his face and strolled over to where Emily still sat on her horse. She studied the young woman for a moment, with a look of concern, and then pointed to her own cheek.

Self-consciously the teacher covered the scratch with her hand. "It's nothing."

With that, the mother turned to her youngest son and began speaking in rapid Norwegian which Emily could not follow. Watching the big man hang his head, she assumed he was being berated for allowing anything to happen to his charge. She couldn't allow that. "He helped me," she blurted out. "Maybe saved my life."


As they sat around the fire that evening, she showed them the knife and told about the Indian.

# 12

"Here comes one! Your side."

The yell from the younger Jones brother, seated at her side on the stand, almost caused Emily to lose her count. Three more head of cattle broke through before Tom closed the gate. The school teacher stood up from the unpadded seat and flexed her stiffened muscles while she watched William turn his horse after the unbranded yearling Andrew had spotted. It was caught by the rider's lariat before it had traveled fifty yards and dragged back to the fire where Franklin sat his on buckskin gelding, waiting. As the young heifer fought the rope around its neck, he lassoed its back legs. Then the two horses, pulling in opposite directions, stretched out the animal so that Hans could push it over on its left side. He sat on its head while Frank stepped off his horse and fetched the red-hot branding iron from the fire. Emily cringed seeing the smoke from the burning hide and smelling the odor of burnt flesh that drifted her way. Then the ropes were removed, the yearling bounded to its feet and ran off. Andrew signalled Tom to open the gate, the woman took her seat, picked up her notebook and the count resumed.

Before the flow of cattle through the gate started again, Emily glanced at the sun and thought it might be early afternoon. In that case, she decided, I've been counting for more than five hours. A rumbling stomach reminded her she hadn't eaten since an early breakfast. Only a couple or three more hours to go, she judged from the size of the herd that remained.

She made marks in her book in groups of five—a short vertical line for each of four animals counted with a fifth represented by a slash through the existing four. That would make adding easier. Three steers rushed past and then there was a brief lull caused by the leaders of the herd trying to turn back. Emily turned to watch Hagen as he strove to keep the cattle moving toward the gate. He had been pressed into service, with some reluctance. A somewhat lazy youth, his usual assignments included helping his mother around the ranch and fulfilling the function of a teamster. He did fine handling horses from the seat of a wagon, but was definitely out of his element astride a horse. Because of the mare's docile nature, Marta had been provided as the young man's mount. The teacher shook her head in exasperation when she saw him hanging onto the side of the saddle after the mare made a quick turn. Tom would have done much better, she thought with a glance at her eleven-year old student standing by the gate. If we weren't more than half done, I'd suggest a change.

Some time later she heard the sound of gunfire coming from downriver. "Who's shooting?" she said to her seat companion.

Andrew chuckled. "Agnus. Ma has her on this side of the other herd to keep 'em from comin' this way. Been there all night. Reckon she caught some sleep in the wagon while Hans looked after the herd." He showed a grin to the young woman at his side. "I'll bet Hans didn't enjoy her company much. She's kinda crabby to be around."

He watched intently the cattle passing below as he talked. "Hans helpin' out here, leaves Agnus to handle the herd herself. Agnus don't move too fast and tryin' to herd cattle from a wagon could be a trial. Reckon some tried to get past her, so she fired off her Winchester. That would discourage 'em like nothin' else."

Andrew stood quickly to check the brand of a yearling, almost hidden behind a big steer. "Now with Ma," he went on after taking his seat, "it'd be a different matter. She took over for Billy this morning to hold 'em at the other end. If any of the stock tried to get past her, she'd be snappin' that big whip of her's and they'd change their thinkin' in a hurry."

"Wouldn't your mother be getting awfully tired and hungry by now? She must have left the ranch quite early in the morning to relieve William. He was here before breakfast." Emily was concerned for the older woman.

"Ma don't know what tired is," he said, "and she always carries grub in her saddle bags."

The youngest Jones brother suddenly stood and yelled to the riders, "Here comes another Bar Vee. It's a heifer. Close the gate, Tom."

Three other cattle from Alf Vik's ranch had come through earlier. With the first, Hans had been consulted and gave his approval. The steer had been caught and had its horns and the top of its head painted red for easy identification later on. The paint had been brought in from the ranch for that purpose.

That raised a question in the teacher's mind. "Why isn't paint used to mark the cattle rather than branding?" she inquired of her pupil.

"Paint would be gone in the spring when the cattle shed their winter coats," he told her.

"No hair ever grows on a brand. That way they're marked for life."

Emily and Andrew watched from the stand as Franklin attempted to paint the big heifer held by William's lariat. Hans, on one side, tried to hold the resisting animal while Franklin approached from the other side. He managed to slop paint on the horns and head but was rewarded for his efforts with a kick in the thigh. He limped away swearing.

"Land sakes! That must have hurt." The look Emily showed the Jones brother at her side was one of concern. "Is he going to be all right?"

"He'll be fine, the big man assured her. "Frank doesn't consider a roundup successful unless he's been kicked a few times. He'll be wearing a black and blue patch for a while."

The teacher marked another "V" on her paper and prepared to continue the count as the gate was opened. The next hour passed quietly.

"This isn't an easy life, is it?" She was thinking aloud, but he turned to look at her.

"It could be worse." His attention was drawn back to the cattle, but he continued talking. "Sure there's some danger and it's hard work at times, but it's rarely dull. Keeps a feller's interest. I couldn't stand a job doin' the same thing over and over, day after day. Could you?" He showed a quick grin. "Women don't take to this life very well, unless they're like Ma. With her, it may be just plain stubbornness. She's determined to make this ranch one of the biggest in the state, if she can. Did you notice how pleased she was with the size of the herd? I reckon she didn't have any idea of how much livestock was here."

"That's not surprising. I wonder if she

knows how much property she has?" Emily said. "How did the ranch get so big, anyway?"

The question appeared to cause Andrew some embarrassment. "Well, I think Pa and Ma played kinda fast and loose with the homestead law. They each got their hundred and sixty acres before they married. Then bought out other settlers who weren't makin' it—sometimes payin' almost nothin'. They had Henny file for another homestead before he had reached legal age. Each of us other brothers have one. They've had other people takin' out homesteads with no intention of usin' the land and then sellin' to the folks. Pa and Ma were purdy shrewd. The homesteads they got hold of circled a big section of the range. Nobody wanted to file for parcels in that area 'cause it would be right in the middle of our ranch. A lot of that range we still don't own, but we use it anyway." Another grin. "I have a hunch Ma is goin' to be askin' you to file for some of that land."

"I won't do it! That's dishonest!"

"Why?"

In her annoyance, she almost forgot her count. "Because I have no intention of staying around for five years to make improvements to the property so it would be mine to sell."

Sensing her increasing anger, he wisely decided to drop the matter. "Billy!" he yelled. "A bull! Tom!"

The boy had been sitting with his back against the fence, half asleep, but he quickly stood and closed the gate.

As the young bull was brought to the fire, Emily turned her head so as not to witness the animal being branded and "fixed".

Only a few cattle remained after the gate

was opened and the count finished quickly. Hans and Tom saddled their horses and hurried to help Frank and William drive the herd through the gap in the buttes and out onto the range beyond.

Before leaving to help his mother bring in the other herd, Andrew gave instructions to Emily and Hagen. "We're goin' to leave the gate open and bunch the herd on this side tonight. Then we'll count them tomorrow going through the same way as today. You two go back where we camped last night and bring the wagon on down to the flat. Build some fires across there. That's where you're goin' to hold the herd. The boys should be back to help, but if they're not, you'll have to do it alone. I should have kept one of the fellers here to give you a hand, but I didn't think about it soon enough." He gave her a questioning look. "Are you sure you can take care of it?"

Emily's lifted chin showed her determination. "Go ahead. We can do it." With that she stepped up onto the saddle and gestured for the youth to climb on behind. And then they were gone.

# 13

The two sat on the mare looking westward. The clouds, that held their attention, were black beneath with pink lofty peaks reflecting the evening sun. They stared in silence for a moment.

"That storm seems headed downriver." She watched nervously, certain that she caught sight of lightning flashing under the base of the clouds. "Think it'll come this way?"

The youth studied the scene over a long period before answering. "Yup." He slipped off Marta and walked over to the two draft horses that were staked out on opposite sides of a pile of hay. A small trough, holding water, was positioned alongside the hay. The length of tether lines barely allowed the horses to reach the water and fodder. Hagen untied one of the two roan geldings and led him to the wagon.

Emily remained seated on the mare as she watched him harness the team. "How long before the storm reaches here?"

"After dark." An expression of concern showed on his face as he glanced again at the clouds.

It wasn't missed by the woman. "Will that be a problem?"

The question caused a degree of discomfort in the young man. It was some time before he answered. "Reckon it can," he said at last.

She wouldn't let the matter alone. "Why is that?"

He paused before fastening the last belly

strap, not wanting to voice the thoughts that his mind produced. "Those longhorns," he said. They're mostly wild and they get scared easy. When they're scared, they run."

Her face blanched. "You mean stampede?" She'd read enough western literature to be familiar with the term as related to cattle.

He nodded, and began hitching the team to the wagon.

"And a lightning strike might cause a stampede." She sat, deep in thought for a while. "We must do everything we can to hold the herd just in case it does stampede. We'd better get to work."

Preparations were nearly complete. The makings for six fires had been set up between the river and the bluff. To save fuel, they elected to wait until the cattle could be heard before lighting the fires. After unloading the wood, Hagen had positioned the wagon behind the line of fires on the side nearest the bluffs. With the horses unhitched and unharnessed, he led them back where they had been previously staked.

Emily decided that it should be her on horseback—she had been witness to Hagen's horsemanship. So mounted, she meant to control a greater section of the line while Hagen, on foot near their camp, would hold responsibility for the remainder. The teacher had taken notice of a Winchester in the wagon and instructed the youth to fire shots in the air, as his mother had done earlier, if needed to stop the herd. Then they settled down to wait.

With time on his hands, Hagen prepared a

roast beef sandwich for each and then, lighting the fire nearest the wagon, began cooking dinner for, what he knew, would be a ravenously hungry group of cattle drovers.

Emily watched nervously as the approaching cloud bank hastened the onset of twilight. She knew it would be dark before the herd arrived and, as she watched another lightning strike and heard the thunder, realized the cattle might very well come charging out of the dark.


Andrew was a worried man. They had finished the count much later than expected. It was hoped that the other herd would have passed through the gate before dark. That, obviously, would not happen. Now there's the weather to reckon with, he thought as he anxiously viewed the western sky.

He'd ridden northeast down the river until he reached the location where a very determined Indian woman was blocking the escape path of the other herd of longhorns. With the Winchester held at arms ready, Agnus had been pacing in front of the line of cattle, a hundred yards away, and they regarded her with apprehension.

While she'd continued her guard duty, Andrew harnessed her team and hitched it to the wagon. It had taken longer than usual since the mare, named Nell, chose that moment to be cantankerous. She was in heat and trying to solicit attention from her teammate, a gelding. Having no comprehension of her needs, he rejected her advances. With ears laid back and teeth bared, he'd fought her off at every turn as the big man tried to attach the traces to the wagon. Finally, in exasperation, he'd brought the mare under control by placing a hard kick to her ribs.

After the woman had climbed to the wagon seat and taken up the reins, the younger Jones brother instructed her to proceed up the river toward the gate and then move the wagon into that gap in the buttes through which the first herd had passed. Sighting a flash of lightning from the approaching storm, he'd given her the same advice as he'd given Emily earlier—to build a line of fires across the opening.

As the light faded, he'd begun to carefully work his way downriver, past the restless cattle, toward the northeast end of the herd where his mother waited.

He found her sitting her mount like a statue—her face grim. In preparation for the expected rain, she'd donned her slicker. He did the same. Then they started the herd moving and he tried to explain the reasons for the delay. She waved off his excuses and galloped away after some stragglers.

The cloud bank moved overhead and Andrew berated himself for leaving his beloved Emily to hold the herd past the gate. Oh Lord help her, he pleaded in silence.

"We'd better light all the fires now," Emily told the young man. "If it starts raining and the wood gets wet, we may not be able to make it burn."

They set about the task immediately and, in time, had a line of blazing fires lighting the evening sky. She mounted the mare, intending to patrol behind the fire line. "Remember," she told Hagen, "if there's a stampede, hide behind the wagon. Don't try to stop the cattle."

And what are you going to do, Emily asked herself, riding away. She had read about cattle stampedes that had taken place in the west, often resulting in cowboys caught up in the herd and trampled to death.

She halted Marta and sat facing northeast—listening. As she watched, a lightning bolt streaked from the cloud cover to the ground. In the minutes that followed, several more strikes occurred. And then one nearby. The instantaneous clap of thunder was deafening. As the sound diminished, it was replaced by another faint rumble that gradually increased in intensity. The mare danced about nervously. She heard Hagen shout a warning and saw him move behind the wagon. At that point she realized the source of the sound. Fear caused her to be incapable of rational thinking. As the roar of pounding hoofs increased, she sat paralyzed. Then she saw the herd emerging from the gloom—saw the firelight reflected on long horns. The mare reacted immediately and whirled to race away, almost losing her rider.

Emily regained her senses and lent herself to the run. Crouched low on the saddle she willed the mare to greater speed. Faster, Marta, faster! The horse stumbled, then caught herself and continued on. Her rider risked a look backward as lightning flashed. The cattle were closer. One thought overwhelmed all others in the woman's mind: If Marta falls, we're dead!

Moonlight showed briefly and Emily realized they were alongside the river. As a steer came abreast the horse, she knew the herd was upon her and, in desperation, she turned Marta to leap into the water. The reins were still in her hand when she surfaced, so she was able to pull herself to the horse and grasp the saddle horn. Around her was the sound of cattle splashing into the river. She had enough presence of mind to rationalize that safety lay downstream behind the herd so she turned the swimming mare in that direction. Although she had dressed in warm clothes, the numbing cold of the water penetrated to her bones. She tried to say words of encouragement to Marta, but her teeth chattered so she could barely speak. The flashes of lightning enabled her to remain oriented with the shoreline where she could see the cattle passing in the rain that was falling in a torrent. When, at last, only a few stragglers remained, she began searching for shallow water where the horse could climb out of the river.

When the stampede began, Andrew's heart almost stopped. In a panic, he tried to race around the herd to reach its head, but could not force his mount through the mass of frantic cattle. Between blinding flashes, he galloped unseeing with the herd until his horse stumbled and fell heavily, rolling on top of the man. His mother rode into the melee, cracking her whip to turn the cattle away from the downed pair. The horse came to its feet, shaken but apparently not suffering serious injury. The big man stood and staggered over to hang on his mother's saddle.

"Oh Ma!" he sobbed. "We've lost her! We've lost her!"

The Jones woman pulled her son's head against her side, bent to kiss his neck and cried with him. A minute passed before the woman straightened in her saddle, pushed the man away and said, "Kom. La oss gå."

When he turned, he noticed the dead yearling that had tripped his mount. As they moved upstream, lightning revealed more dead cattle—usually young stock. Through the pouring rain they spotted the line of fires, off to the left, that Agnus had set. Approaching the camp, where Andrew had left her at the break in the buttes, they found the Indian woman standing behind a fire, rifle in hand. It was obvious that none of the herd had ventured near the formidable figure.

The team was still hitched to the wagon, so Karen Jones simply waved her to follow. A kerosene lantern hung from the wagon and provided barely adequate light, in the downpour, for them to make their way along the river. They passed without stopping where the fence and gate had stood. Both were broken and knocked flat on the ground. Andrew could see the Indian woman's face by the light of the lantern. Her expression was stoic, although he realized the torment she was suffering with concern for her son. He had his own pain.

They found the other wagon by following the line of scattered firewood. The rain had quenched all the flames. Their first sighting of the wreckage brought cries from both women. The wagon box was upside down with one wheel missing. A dead young heifer lay on top. There was a trail of debris that followed the passage of the herd. Agnus pulled her team to a halt and looked around frantically. In a plaintive voice she called out her son's name, but the sound was lost in the raging storm. Andrew stepped off his horse and surveyed the battered heap. Shaking his head in frustration, he kicked the wagon box. He fell back in shock when he heard a muffled yell and an answering thump come from the box. Quickly he dragged off the dead animal and, with a massive effort, rolled the wagon onto its side. Hagen extracted himself from the clutter of cooking materials, bedding, assorted clothing, hay, harnesses and tools. When he stood up, his mother gave a squeal of delight and climbed down from her seat to embrace her son.

"Ma!" he said. "I'm getting all wet."

Agnus laughed and hustled him inside her covered wagon.

As Andrew remounted his horse, his mother grabbed the reins. "Hvor skal du gå?"

"To look for Emily!" He tried to pull the horse away from her grasp.

"Nei! nei!" She held on with determination. "Du må vente til det blir lyst."

"I'll use Agnus's lantern for light."

"Nei!" Her next words were a command that could not be dismissed. "Kom ned! Du må vente!"

"Ma!" he pleaded, "I can't wait!"

She took hold of his arm. "Kom," she said gently.

He yielded with a sob and climbed down from the horse.

The mother put her arms around her youngest son and patted him on the back. "Det vil gå fint"

"It can't be fine unless she's alive," he protested.

"Nei! Stopp nå! Vi skal finne henne i

morgen," she said firmly. "Nå hjelpe Agnus tenne brann. Stort brann!" She pushed him away and he went with Agnus and Hagen to gather some of the scattered wood to make a fire—a big fire.

After they had placed a pile of the wet logs behind the overturned wagon, which served as a windbreak, the Indian woman brought out a can of kerosene from her wagon and poured a liberal amount over the wood. She used her lantern to ignite a splinter, soaked with fuel, and start the fire. While his mother and Hagen collected more logs, Andrew took some rope and a canvas tarp from Agnus's wagon. Using the wagon wreckage, along with two leftover fence poles, he fashioned a crude shelter.

Afterward, he positioned the other wagon near the fire, unhitched the team and used it to drag away the carcass of the heifer. Then he unharnessed the team, unsaddled his own and his mother's horses, and staked the animals where they could reach a pile of hay.

The activity was not enough to keep him distracted from thoughts of his adored Emily and tears mixed with the rain on his face.

As Agnus was preparing food, two other Jones brothers rode in. "We saw what was left of the fence," Franklin said, dismounting. "Was anybuddy hurt?"

No one answered. Then Karen gave her son a brief hug. "Hvor er de andre?"

"The others?" It was a moment before he could tear his attention away from the surrounding disorder and answer his mother. "Zachary thought he better get the boys out of the storm." He looked at the four other faces, confused by their sullen expressions. "They're over at the ranch. They'll come out in the mornin'."

Hagen walked into the firelight, carrying an armful of wood.

"Well howdy there, ol' hoss," Franklin greeted the youth. "I see you got outta the way. Where's your partner?" He knew the answer immediately—sorrow showed in the youth's eyes before he ducked his head.

"She got caught? How did that happen?"

Andrew looked at his brother. "I left her here. I should've known better."

"They ran!" Hagen blurted out. "She was on Marta. They ran." He shook his head, remembering. "The herd was right behind. After the fires went out I didn't see no more. And then the cattle hit the wagon and knocked it over on me."

Franklin stared in disbelief. "You wasn't hurt?"

"Not much." The youth looked at the battered remains of the wagon, laying on its side. "Knocked it clear over on me. I was inside the box. Covered over—tangled up. I couldn't get out until Andrew turned it over."

Franklin reached out and put his hand on the young man's shoulder. "You was lucky, Hoss. You can tell your grandkids you lived through a stampede. Not everbuddy can say that."

"I don't think Miss O'Neal was that lucky," William muttered with his head lowered. He looked up to see the scowls on the faces of the others. "I mean she might be...she could...well, the mare ain't too fast..." He suddenly decided he'd said enough and clamped his mouth closed.

"Det er min feil." Everyone turned to look at Karen Jones who stood with tears streaming. "Jeg sa hun skulle gjøre det."

95

The youngest son stood closest to his mother and he took her in his arms. "No, Ma," he sobbed. "You're not to blame. She wanted to ride. It gave her great pleasure. Emily would tell you that if she was here."

Franklin was looking beyond the fire and his eyes widened. "You mean that Emily?" he said pointing.

Marta walked slowly out of the darkness into the firelight, her rider, thoroughly spent, was hunched over clinging to the saddle horn.

The brothers rushed to her aid. While Franklin and William pulled her feet from the stirrups, Andrew gently lifted her from the saddle. His mother rushed forward to grab him by the sleeve and guide him to the covered wagon. There he surrendered his responsibility to the care of the two older women, and was promptly shooed away. Emily was quickly stripped of her sopping wet clothing, dried and wrapped in a blanket. Then the big man was summoned again to carry the exhausted woman to the fire.

And all night long Andrew sat under the shelter, holding his warmed and sleeping teacher in his arms. It didn't seem possible he could ever let her go.

# 14

The storm ended during the night. At daybreak, members of the cheerless little camp began to stir. Most had only brief periods of sleep. Franklin and William had shared the duty of maintaining the fire. Otherwise they sat and dozed, on one side of their big brother and his assumed ward. Their mother had guarded the other side.

Emily slept with her head on his chest, like a child. Her face was slack in repose, showing no awareness of the violence that had occurred overnight. Andrew wanted to hold the lovely young woman forever. He noticed that his mother was awake and watching. They smiled at each other.

Franklin was the first to move. He stood, grumbling and swearing under his breath while rubbing his sore leg. After placing a couple of logs on the fire's embers, he hobbled to the other side of Agnus's wagon to urinate.

The Indian woman emerged from the back end of the covered wagon carrying a coffee pot which she filled with water from the wooden keg strapped to the wagon's side. She said her son's name sharply and brought the pot to the fire.

William groaned and rolled over onto his knees. He retrieved his hat and came to his feet. When he looked around and saw the carcasses of cattle dotting the landscape, he made a sour face. "Bet we lost fifty head," he said to his mother.

Karen Jones nodded and arose. She

walked to the wagon tongue, that had been swung near the fire and propped up to serve as a drying rack. Emily's clothing had dried, to the Jones woman's satisfaction, so were carried to the covered wagon and tossed inside. "Kom ut der fra," she told the youth.

Emily awoke and looked around confused. When she realized she had been sleeping in the big man's arms, she gave him a shy smile and moved slightly. It was then she became aware she had nothing on under the blanket and gasped aloud. The Jones woman took notice and beckoned for her youngest son to bring his teacher to the wagon. With his brothers' help, Andrew stood and, on wobbly legs, carried Emily to the back of the wagon.

"Hagen!" he said in a voice of authority, "Get outta there!"

Two boots and a hat came flying out from inside followed by the tousle-headed young man, trying to hold his coat and button his shirt at the same time.

"Your clothes are inside," Andrew told the young woman as he placed her gently on the wagon's tail gate. "I think they're dry."

She smiled her thanks and gave him a quick kiss on the cheek before rolling inside and closing the canvas flaps.

The big man blushed and looked at his mother. He thought he detected a knowing smile before she turned away.

When Emily joined the others at the fire, and was handed a tin cup full of coffee, she stood looking over the flat toward the river. "So many dead," she said, her eyes filling with tears, "and it's all my fault. If I hadn't insisted on a count, they'd be alive."

"Nei, nei." The older woman made a motion with her hand as if brushing away the dead cattle."

"Good God!" Franklin spoke up. "That's nothin'."

"Franklin!" his mother admonished.

"Sorry, Ma." he said automatically. "A lot of winters we lose more than that, but then ever' spring we get three or four hundred calves to keep us ahead of the game."

The others nodded.

William looked at the young woman. He couldn't hold the question any longer. "How did you get away?"

"We jumped into the river." She scowled at the recollection. "I hung onto the saddle and Marta swam downstream. There were cattle falling into the water all around us. I have no idea how many. After the herd passed and the lightning flashed again, Marta saw a place where she could climb the bank to get out of the river. I would never have found it. I was so cold." Remembering caused her to shiver in spite of the heat from the fire. "Marta saved my life. I could barely climb up in the saddle afterward. I don't know how she found her way here."

Her listeners sipped their coffee in silence.

Emily looked at Hagen and smiled. "I was so happy to see you alive. How did you escape?"

He pointed at the wrecked wagon. "I was under that."

"And you weren't hurt?"

"Not much," he said bravely.

She looked again at the shambles around her and then, again, at the dead cattle out on the flat. "So much danger," she said quietly. "So much loss."

"Some of them cattle probably got out of the river," William said. "Reckon we'll find 'em downstream a piece."

"Ain't as bad as it looks," the youngest brother put in. "I can fix up this ol' wagon. Fact is, I think I see the wheel down yonder." He started walking in the direction the herd had taken. The others watched as he covered the ground in long strides. When he reached the wheel and picked it up, they could see part of the wooden structure still attached.

"Only one broken spoke," he said upon rejoining the group. "Hub and rim are fine. I'll wire this on the frame to get the empty wagon back to the ranch. Have it fixed up like new for you in a few days," he told the young man with a grin.

Hagen didn't appear especially pleased.

While the conversation had been going on, Agnus busied herself preparing breakfast. She'd set up a grill over the fire's embers and had eggs and bacon frying on a big skillet. A pan of bread rolls warmed next to the flames. The members of her hungry audience were handed tin plates full of food and, while they set about devouring the contents with unabashed gusto, the Indian woman cooked more. She and her son were the last to eat.

Franklin released a lasting belch. "Reckon we better start roundin' 'em up in the mornin'. Get one good night's sleep, anyway."

"Zachary can help you," William told his older sibling. "I'll go on down river and bring back what's there."

"I'll start puttin' up the fence and gate again," Andrew said. "Shouldn't take more than a couple of days."

Emily took all of it in, her face showing astonishment. "You can't mean you're going ahead and finish the count?"

"Of course," Franklin said. "Hell!...sorry Ma...we can't let a little thing like a stampede keep us from doin' our work."

"The school teacher looked at the older woman. "Is this what you want?"

"Ja. Det blir bra."

"But..." The young woman's head was swimming. What does it take to stop these people, she wondered.

Franklin grinned mischievously. "You can't get out of a job that easy."

The whole situation was ridiculous to the point that it caused her to burst out laughing, which surprised those around. "Well partner," she said, turning to Andrew and holding out her hand, "it looks like you're stuck with me again."

That didn't disappoint the big man at all.

# 15

The count finished on Saturday afternoon without further incident. Emily gave her hostess the final tally at the dinner table that evening. She read from a little red notebook. "Two-thousand, three-hundred and seventeen. We marked fifteen head of Bar Vee stock to be returned." The teacher lowered her voice with the next announcement. "I'm sorry to say we lost at least thirty-six head—more may have drowned in the river and been carried downstream. William found sixteen that were able to swim ashore."

Karen Jones seemed satisfied and smiled. "Dat vas good," she said in her broken English.

Emily wondered how the older woman could be so casual about the loss of her livestock. "Now," she told the gathering, "I will need to know about every animal that's been sold or died. Also a count must be kept of every one branded...," she glanced at Andrew, ..."whether it belongs to the ranch or not."

Franklin interrupted. "How will we know how many died? Some are killed by wolves. Coyotes get some of the young stock. Others freeze over the winter." He looked around the table at his mother and brothers. "Sometimes we don't find what's left of 'em."

The teacher sat for a moment—thinking. "What do you do with the dead when you find them?"

"What do you think?" he scoffed. "We don't eat 'em."

"Franklin!" his mother warned.

He grinned at his brothers. "We don't even give 'em a proper burial." He accepted another slap from his mother.

Emily couldn't conceal her smile. "I wouldn't imagine you would, but we must try to keep track of the cattle as best we can to show accountability?"

"Account-a-what?" he said.

"To show that its death had been noted. Otherwise it might be counted several times."

Franklin looked at his mother. "Is that what you want us to spend our time doin'? Countin' dead cattle? Then what?" He looked at the younger woman. "Bury em'? We could spend half a day digging a hole big enough to bury the carcass and then the critters would dig it up durin' the night."

Karen Jones nodded toward the teacher. "Hør på henne."

He doesn't want to listen to anyone, Emily thought. Particularly me. She was becoming somewhat irritated with the third Jones son. "There must be some way you could mark the location of the dead animal. Form a square around it with a little pile of rocks or a stake at each of four corners. It might take five minutes."

Franklin shook his head. "We'll have stakes and little piles of rocks all over this ranch. I don't see why we need that."

"For a very good reason," she told him. "The more accurate we are in keeping the records, the better idea we'll have of the ranch's assets." She showed a little smile. "And we may not need to do another count for a long time."

Emily was carrying the little red notebook as she approached the youngest brother. Andrew had the damaged wagon turned upside down and was replacing the broken frame member that supported the axle. "Still doin' the inven..."

"Inventory. I need your help for a while."

She was wearing a simple print dress that clung to her slim figure like bark on a tree. Her face was shaded by a broad-brimmed hat, with a bright green ribbon for a hat band. There was no way he could ever deny her request. She crooked her finger and he followed her into the barn.

"These stacks of lumber," she indicated with a wave of her hand, "how much is here?"

"Quite a few board-feet, I reckon."

A little frown showed on her face. "Board-feet?"

"Yup. That's what Pa called it." The big man removed his hat to wipe his forehead. "That's a board twelve inches wide by twelve inches long and an inch thick."

"But these boards are all different widths and thicknesses." She studied the pile of lumber. "We'll just measure the stack for an approximation. Can you get a ruler?"

He produced a yardstick from near by. "Will this do?"

She nodded. "How wide is the stack?"

He measured. "Eight feet and eight inches."

"There's some spaces between boards so we'll say eight feet even." She walked the length of the stack. "The boards aren't all the same length, either." She eyed the ends of the stack. "Let's measure from here...," she marked a board with her pencil, "...to here." She made another mark near the opposite end of the same board.

"That's an average length."

"About eleven feet and three inches," he said.

She wrote in her book. "Multiplying eight by eleven and a quarter gives us ninety square feet. How high is the stack?"

"Seven feet and seven inches," he told her.

"But there's spaces between the boards. Why is that?"

"So the wood'll dry." He grinned at the young woman. "It's kinda green when we saw it into boards."

"Very well," she said. "We'll use just half the height—about forty-five inches. Multiply by ninety...," she wrote some figures in her book, "...is four-thousand and fifty board feet." She looked pleased with herself.

Andrew was in awe of his teacher.

"This is an approximation, but it's good enough. Now let's measure the other stacks."

Emily wanted to know everything. As she wandered around the ranch, the big man and his yardstick in tow, she questioned him incessantly. "What did this cost? How much grain in here? How many chickens? How much hay?" They measured and counted for most of the afternoon.

Later, as they sat on the overturned wagon, she asked the more difficult questions. "How much lumber do you trade for a steer? Or for hay?"

He scratched his head. "That depends."

"On what?"

"If it's a prime steer and we want it. If we have a lot of lumber or not much. If we need the hay." He grinned. "If it's a good friend or somebody we don't like very much."

"Oh," she said, eyebrows raised. "And who

is it you don't like very much?  Bull Bjornson?"

"Nah."  The big man chuckled.  "Bull's all right.  A little rough around the edges when he's drunk, but a good friend.  We don't care much for Noel Cuthbertson."

"Who is Noel Cuthbertson?"

"Noel owns the spread next to ours over on the southeast side," he said.

"What's wrong with him?" Emily persisted.

Andrew ducked his head—embarrassed. "He's a bachelor and his treatment of young ladies ain't too pleasin' to folks around here."

"What do you mean?"

"He's a little too...er...forward," the Jones man said.

"He flirts?"

"Worse than that.  A couple of gals said he tried to take advantage of them.  Their dads have threatened to shoot him on sight if they catch him bothering their girls."  He hesitated, his face coloring, before he spoke again.  "Folks are saying that something happened with Missus Adams' daughter.  You know her, don't you?  She works with her mother in that little cafe.  There's something wrong with the girl, up here."  He tapped his forehead.  "Missus Adams won't talk about what happened.  She's a widow, you know, so there's not much she could do, anyway.  People are wondering if the girl is in a family way."  He let loose an embarrassed cough.

"My word!"  Emily showed a look of astonishment.  "Why don't folks do something about him?"

"Can't," Andrew said.  "The girl isn't goin' to say nothin' ...er...anything, so where's the proof?"

"That's terrible!"  Green eyes blazed.  "The Jones family certainly doesn't condone that type of behavior."

"We don't do him any favors."

"Well I should hope you wouldn't." The teacher sat quietly thinking for a moment, then collected herself. "We'd better get back to the business at hand. So, am I to assume that all transactions take place by barter?"

"Bart...? Reckon so."

"Well," she said with resignation, "this place isn't exactly the general store. You don't do much trading with money?"

"Not a lot. Most folks around here don't have much money, except for some in town."

She pursed her lips—thinking. "But your family has money, what with all the cattle you sell for shipping back east. I'll have to check with the bank to find out the status of your account."

A burst of laughter came from the big man. "You won't find any of our money in the bank."

"Land sakes! Why not?"

"Ma don't like Henry Cotter." He was still grinning.

Emily shook her head. "Why would she allow her personal dislike of the bank owner to influence her need for prudent monetary management?"

He didn't answer—merely sat frowning.

She recognized the intimation. "I mean she should have some form of accounting for her money. Where does she keep it, anyway?"

"In a box in her room. She just puts money in when she gets it and takes it out when she needs it."

The teacher was aghast. "In a box—just sitting there! It could be taken or lost or burn or blow away." Unconcern over money was not to be found in the young woman's range of disposition.

"How much does she have?"

He shrugged. "Who knows?  Only her and Agnus ever go into her room.  Reckon Ma don't know neither."

"But that money is part of the ranch's assets.  It's got to be included in the inventory."

"She'll never let you see it," he said.

But he was wrong.


When Emily posed the question to the older woman after the evening meal, Karen Jones took the teacher by the hand and led her into her room. "Der!"  she said, opening the box. "Count!"

# 16

"I worry about you having to ride all the way back to the ranch at night, Emily told the big man."

They sat side by side at the table in Missus Larson's dining room. "It gets dark so early this time of year, and if the weather turns bad, you could get lost and freeze to death."

She had never expressed concern for his safety before, and it gave him a good feeling. "I'm goin' to be fine," he said smiling. "There's a full moon out tonight and most of the snow is gone. The horse knows the way home even if I forget."

"But it's so far."

Andrew shook his head. "Naw. Only about five miles. Get ol' Dagger trottin', it's less than an hour."

"I've been meaning to ask, why do you call your horse' Dagger?"

"Oh, that. Have you ever noticed that white spot on his forehead? Called a star. Billy thought it was shaped like a dagger, so that's what we named 'im." Andrew was greatly relieved to be able to carry on a conversation with his teacher in an easy, relaxed manner. He remembered his frustration, during their earlier times together, when he hardly dared to speak. That problem ended during the roundup. Since the night he held her by the fire, there had been a special bond formed and for that he loved her even more.

She smiled at her pupil. "When I see him

again, I'm going to look more closely for the dagger." Her expression became serious. "But what will you do if the weather turns bad?"

"If it's that bad, I won't be showin' up." He couldn't imagine storms so severe that he could be kept from spending time with his adored teacher. "If it starts to kick up while I'm here after dark, reckon I'll just bed down at the livery. I've got my bedroll with my saddle."

She looked at him wide eyed. "The livery! Land sakes! Why would you do that? I'm sure Missus Larson could find some place for you to sleep."

"Nope. Wouldn't want to put her to any bother. I've slept there before—lots of us fellers have." He showed his embarrassment. "That's where we usually end up after a Saturday night dance. Sometimes we ain't fit to ride home."

She remembered the night at the dance when he had so nobly defended her honor. "Well, if you need to stay over again, I hope you'll let me try to make some arrangements with Missus Larson. A man shouldn't be sleeping with animals."

"Why not?" he said. "They keep the place nice and warm. Better than sleeping with a herd of longhorns out on the prairie." He gave her a wink.

That brought out her laugh, which he loved to hear. "I suppose you're right about that. Well don't expect me to sleep in a livery with you." She suddenly realized the words she had spoken and blushed profusely. When she saw his face redden, she laughed again. "I can't believe I said that."

He joined in the fun. "I can't believe I heard it."

"Before this gets worse, we'd better get back to the lesson," she said picking up the book.


Emily was amazed at the rapid progress he had made in reading. She judged him to be at about ninth grade level, which had presented his teacher with the problem of supplying him enough books. She remembered that Henrik had a great many books in his room and requested permission of Karen Jones to look over her absent son's personal library. That had nearly brought about another confrontation with the mother but, in the end, she grudgingly consented. At that time her student was reading two or three books each week.

"Why so much?" He'd been bothered by the extensive reading assignments. "So many words I don't know. I'm practically sleepin' with Webster's dictionary as it is."

"English is a very complicated language," she'd told him, "especially here in America. Because we've borrowed so many words from other languages, we now have the biggest vocabulary, by far. Don't be disappointed if you're not learning all the words. No one ever does. There are words that are pronounced the same as other words, but spelled differently. In some instances, several words have the same spelling but different pronunciations. And, of course, these similar words all have different meanings, depending on context and usage.

"Many languages, like Spanish, have rules for spelling and pronunciation that are quite consistent. We have some rules, but there are so many exceptions to the rules that the rules become meaningless. It's simpler to memorize the individual words and you'll get that through reading and hearing proper English spoken. That's why we talk so much. People learn a spoken language by hearing it from the time they're born. They simply mimic the speaker. If they learn from those who use improper language, that's what they'll speak. You've been listening, for too long, to the speech of your father and other folks around here. Now I want you to listen to me. It's taken me many years of high quality education to achieve a good command of the English language, so if you learn to speak as I do, you'll do very well."

Emily was pleased that he applied himself with diligence. He still tended to shorten words with an "ing" ending, but that was gradually changing. The extensive reading was helping him organize his thoughts into better sentence structure. To avoid being teased by his brothers, he continued to use the local vernacular when talking with them, but in conversations with his teacher, he tried to copy her speech. She never failed to poke fun at him for his "quaint" expressions such as: "...mad as a March hare," or, "... quick as greased lightning".

Quite recently, she had begun mathematics instruction. He learned quickly how to add columns of numbers and how to perform substraction. After she had explained that "multiplication" was simply multiple additions, he was made aware of the benefits gained by memorizing the multiplication table through number twelve. Division was somewhat more difficult, but soon mastered. Fractions, involving a numerator and a denominator, and decimal fractions, caused his head to spin. Teacher and pupil sat together for hours, poring over the problems until the big man had realized full understanding.

Emily worried about teaching higher mathematics—algebra, geometry and calculus. Her own background wasn't that strong. We'll just have to deal with it when we reach that point, she decided.

Much to his surprise, the younger Jones brother enjoyed history and civics. His teacher believed, emphatically, that those subjects should be given life, rather than being relegated to collections of names, events and dates. She tried to make her student acquainted with the individuals and places involved. Using maps, they followed Hannibal's march from Spain, across the Rhone River and the Alps, in his quest to capture Rome. They studied English law to learn how it applied to the Constitution and the Bill of Rights. The teacher gathered all information available concerning the seventh president of the United States and Andrew's namesake, Andrew Jackson. She told her pupil that Jackson was called "Old Hickory" by the men in his army because of his toughness. "He was quite a disreputable figure," she'd said with a grin. "Hard drinking, fighting, argumentative fellow. Killed a man in a dual. It was said that the man insulted Jackson's wife, a beautiful woman who'd been married before."

In her first winter in Montana, Emily found that Franklin hadn't been stretching the truth by much. It was cold. The temperature at night often dropped to twenty degrees below zero. Her usual routine was to rise early and, still wrapped in her bedding, make a fire in the room's little stove and put on a pan of water. Then she would dash back to bed to remain until the room and water had warmed enough to risk washing and dressing. By that time, Missus Larson would have breakfast set out in the dining room. Back in her room after breakfast, she would brush her teeth and tend to her other needs. Afterwards, bundled like an Eskimo and, in her long boots, she would begin the trek through the snow on up the hill to the schoolhouse.

Inside she would light a lantern and kindle the stove. Still in her warm clothing, she would begin grading papers and preparing for the day's lessons. Shortly before nine o'clock the children would arrive—those who braved the weather—and education would resume.

At three o'clock, the boys in the class would be assigned the task of carrying in the next day's supply of firewood from the shed out back. The girls chores consisted of gathering slates, papers and books from the tables and placing those in the cabinet. After the general confusion of children donning their warm clothing, saying good-byes and filing out the door, their teacher would remain working at her desk until the fire had died and the room became chilly.

Then she would put on her own outer garments and boots, trudge back down the hill to the boarding house for supper and to await the arrival of Andrew Jones.

Friday afternoon the routine would be altered somewhat. If the weather permitted, she would dismiss the children early and find Andrew waiting for her outside with the buckboard. He would take her to the boarding house to collect those items needed at the ranch, and they would start on the long drive.

Sunday afternoon, unless a storm was brewing, she would return to start the week again.

# 17

"I was beginning to think spring would never come."

Sunday morning Emily stood with her pupil on the ranch house porch looking out over the prairie. Only a little snow remained and some green sprouts were starting to show. Far to the southwest they could see the faint white outline of the Big Snowy Mountains showing through the clear crisp air. "Such a long winter. Does it always last until May?"

"Nope," he said. "Sometimes it ends in April." He smiled at the young woman. "We usually get a spring and summer if we wait around long enough."

"I don't know if I can tolerate another winter." She shivered in her sheepskin coat. "It's so cold."

Andrew felt the ache that always accompanied thoughts of her going away. "Folks get used to it," he said. "Besides, you can't leave this year. You wanted to see the newest state added to the union. Remember?"

She showed a wry expression. "Yes, I remember. I suppose I'd better stay around for that. They're saying in town that congress is considering that Omnibus Bill I was telling you about. Montana is intended to be one of the four states."

"Let's see." He rubbed his chin, thinking. "It was with North and South Dakotas and ..."

"Washington," she said.

"That's right. Washington."

"Probably won't take place until late in the year or the first part of next." A rueful little smile appeared. "Guess I'll be stuck here for another winter."

The big man breathed a sigh of relief. "Next winter might not be as bad."

"And it might be worse. Oh well," she said with resignation, "at least this one is over. Should be much easier traveling back and forth to town." She looked closely at the man. "I suggested to your mother that I could make the trip by myself if she would let me keep a horse at the livery in town during these last weeks of school. I'm sure I know the way by now. She told me to take Marta."

The big man looked distraught. He would miss being in her company an extra two or three hours a week. "I don't know..." He tried to produce an argument. "Might be dangerous. Could still be some Indians hanging around."

Remembering her encounter with the young Indian during the roundup caused her face to pale slightly. "There aren't supposed to be any left in this area. We've never seen any between here and Broken Wagon."

"You don't see Indians if they don't want to be seen." His voice carried with it an ominous warning.

"I'm sure I'd be fine." She seemed uncertain. "But it's not right that you should waste five or six hours a week bringing me here and back." She saw the worried expression on his face. "You have an extra pistol I could take along with me, don't you?"

"Yes, but you don't know how to shoot."

"Then teach me," she said firmly. "Right

now."

"Right now?" He saw in her that same determination she'd shown when learning to ride. "I...er...don't think..."

"Right now!" she said again.

"Alright, if you're sure it's what you want." He started for the front door and stopped. "Ma bought a little thirty-two caliber Smith and Wesson last year. It doesn't kick like the Colt thirty-eight she usually carries." He went inside and returned a few minutes later carrying the weapon. "Here's a holster for it. You'd get tired carrying it in your hand and it's no use to you in a saddlebag where you can't get to it in a hurry. We'd better go out behind the barn."

Emily looked at the gun with some distaste. "Perhaps I'd better change into my riding clothes. I don't want to dirty my dress."

"Now, what do I do" She was wearing her denim trousers and a homespun cotton shirt under her coat. She also had on her boots and the western hat. The gun holster was strapped around her waist.

Andrew thought she looked particularly fetching. "I set up some cans on the fence over there," he said, pointing. "Take out the gun and point it in that direction."

The teacher showed her apprehension as she aimed the gun toward the fence.

"It's better if you use two hands in the beginning." He showed her the proper grip. "Now hold your arms straight out in front. Look along the barrel and line up the two sights. This tab is the front sight...," he put his finger on the tab,

"...and it should fit into the notch on the back sight. Can you hold it there?"

She did as she was told, and nodded.

"Good. Now lower the gun down. Point toward the ground out in front and rest your arms for a minute." He grinned encouragement. "No reason to be scared. You'll do fine."

A frown of concern showed on her face.

"Don't worry," he said. "I'll talk you through each step. Ready?"

She nodded.

"Fine. Take your finger off the trigger and lift the gun. That's right. Don't touch the trigger. Pull back the hammer until it clicks. Now line up the sights on a can and put your finger on the trigger, but don't pull it. Hold it steady and gradually squeeze the trigger."

He could see the gun barrel wavering slightly and then the revolver discharged. Emily jumped with the blast of sound and shock of the weapon recoiling in her hands.

"Whoa!" he said. "Keep the gun pointing out that way."

"The can!" she said, letting loose a squeal of delight. "It's gone! Where is it?"

"It's rolling out across the prairie somewhere."

"I hit it! My first try and I hit it!" She looked at him eagerly. "Let's do it again."

She did it again. And again. And again.

After he had shown her how to reload the gun, he gave her pockets full of cartridges and walked away. "Gotta tend to the horses," he told her.

All morning long he heard the gun discharging, with interruptions that suggested she was setting up more cans.

It was nearly noon, while he was repairing a pitchfork handle, that she walked up to him—the gun in her holster. "No more bullets," she told him.

He stood silently studying her, a big grin on his face.

"What?" she said.

"I wish I had two photographs of you, the way you look right now."

Unconsciously her hand went to the hair that showed under her hat. "Why? What would you do with them."

"I'd keep one and send the other to your parents."

"You'd do what?" She looked at him in astonishment—her mouth gaping.

"Sure," he said. "What would they think of their college-educated daughter, seeing her like this?"

Emily let out a shriek of laughter. "My mother would die! She'd know I've become another Calamity Jane. I'd hear her scream all the way from New York." A wicked gleam came into her eye. "It's a shame there isn't a photographer around here."

He chuckled. "There is."

"There is?" she said. "Who?"

"Milt Jensen. He does it mostly as a hobby. Sells a few pictures now and then, but it's not a living. It's like the little newspaper he prints. You've seen it?"

"Oh yes. It's called 'The Wagon Spoke'." She wrinkled her nose. "Fancy."

"Doesn't make anything off that, either, but he says he has fun. Folks aren't too pleased about some of the things he prints, but that doesn't seem to bother him."

"How does he make a living?" He had stirred her interest.

"Got a business out near the livery. Sells and repairs saddles and harnesses. Also owns a little spread south of town where he runs a few hundred head."

"Would he photograph me?"

The big man snickered. "Why he'd fall all over himself to make a picture of you, especially in that get-up."

"Would he do it today?"

"He would if I asked him. I've done him some favors."

"Well lets go, then." She turned away. "I'll get my things."

He decided to tease her. "I thought you wanted to go alone."

She grinned. "No. You'd better come with me the first time to make sure I don't shoot somebody."

# 18

"He's selling those pictures all over town. How could you let him do such a thing?"

The big man couldn't help but grin. "Wasn't my doing."

Emily had seen her pupil arrive and came out into the street in front of the boarding house to meet him. She didn't want Missus Larson to overhear their conversation.

"But he's your friend."

"Probably didn't think it would do any harm. Marv is something of a renegade. Does things his own way." Andrew was slow to notice that his teacher was deeply disturbed. She seemed close to tears. "Is it that bad?"

She turned away from him and dabbed her eyes with a handkerchief. He resisted an urge to hold and comfort the young woman.

"Frida brought one of the pictures to show the class," she said still facing away. "I suppose that Tom and Hans have told the other students about my involvement in the roundup, but a picture makes it so...so conspicuous. I heard one of the children say I looked like Cattle Anne. Who is Cattle Anne?"

He grimaced at the question. "As I remember, her name was McDougal. Her and a friend, they called Little Britches, were cattle rustlers. They may have been hung, for all I know. That's been the usual treatment for rustlers in some parts."

"That's terrible!" she cried. "Cattle rustlers!

No wonder they laughed. It's difficult enough trying to maintain discipline in a classroom without being made the butt of jokes. And then Mister Cotter came by last evening. He told me I'd made a spectacle of myself and said that the mothers of some of the girls had complained of my behavior." She sniffed. "They thought a woman teacher should set a better example for the children."

Andrew couldn't think of anything to say.

"He also said they would take up the issue at the next meeting of the school board. I had no idea that such an innocent act could cause such an uproar."

"They're making too much of a fuss over this," he said. "I wouldn't let it worry me if I was you. Ma will keep the school board in line."

"But it's so embarrassing. Can't you stop Mister Jensen from selling those pictures?"

She couldn't see his grin. "A little late for that. I imagine everyone who wants one, has it by now."

"Please," she said.

"I'll talk to him. Now, hadn't we better go inside?" he said. "Missus Larson is peeking out the window."


## THE WAGON SPOKE
### THE VOICE OF BROKEN WAGON & VICINITY
MAY 16, 1889   5 CENTS   PROP: MARVIN T. JENSEN


On occasion the editor feels it is his civic duty to pay tribute to a member of the community whose special contributions have added to the safety and well being of the citizens of Broken Wagon and surrounding areas. That particular individual is none other than our own Henry J. Cotter, owner of the Broken Wagon Bank and other properties. Through his diligence, the community can feel much more secure and sleep better at night. For it was Mister Cotter who recognized the imminent danger represented by the appearance of the sinister figure, who appeared on our street, dressed as a derelict drifter and wearing a six-shooter. Henry immediately took the necessary steps to protect the bank and the savings of the good people hereabout. There being no sheriff in our town, Mister Cotter, unarmed, took it upon himself to approach and warn the scoundrel to be on good behavior or risk the possibility of expulsion. Had this person chosen to commit wrongdoing, I'm quite sure that our stouthearted banker would have led the posse in pursuit (had he been able to fit his more than ample girth into a saddle). Thankfully this proved unnecessary. The ruffian chose, instead, to submit meekly and return to the classroom. The town will be relieved to learn that a schoolteacher (unnamed) will leave her weapon at home, no matter how threatening the children.

"I wish I'd never gone to town dressed like that. Your friend's paper has made me a laughing-stock." She sat looking out over the prairie and sighed. "Before that I was viewed as somewhat eccentric. Now I'm a figure of ridicule."

Andrew shifted his chair on the ranch

house porch so he could lean it back against the building. "I didn't know he was going to do that. It was never mentioned." He showed her a grin. "If it makes you feel any better, your embarrassment is nothing compared with what Henry Cotter is going through right now. He hardly dare show his face in town. Another thing, now you can ride into town as Lady Godiva, if you want, and you'll never hear a peep out of him."

Emily had to laugh. "You don't believe I'd be more of a sensation than before?"

"Well," he said. "You'd be traveling lighter and cooler."

"That's a careful answer if I ever heard one." She paused for a moment, a frown showing. "I'm debating whether I should continue riding to town or not. I do enjoy it."

"Then keep doing it. Ma would be very disappointed if you quit."

"Your mother?" The teacher was puzzled. "Why would she care one way or another?"

"Because they can't stop her from doing anything she wants to do. She rides her horse into town as often as she drives the buckboard. It's just a matter of whether she'll be picking up more than she can carry back in her saddle bags." He interrupted his oratory with a chuckle. "She does what she feels like doing. No one ever knows what that will be. Now then," he scratched his head, "what was the question? Oh yes. Why should she care? I think she looks at you as a duplicate of herself. She likes your spirit. I don't think you'd want to let her down."

"I could never be the woman she is," the teacher grinned at the big man, "but I suppose that shouldn't stop me from trying."

Emily knew she would go to great lengths to

keep the respect of Karen Jones. "No," she told the big man. I can't let your mother down."

With that, she suddenly stood, pulled the pistol from her holster and twirled it around her finger. "Look out, Broken Wagon," she said with a laugh. "I'll be a comin' to town, six-shooter and all."

"That's my girl," he said, matching her laugh.

"Your girl? Since when am I your girl?"

"Whoa!" he said. "Wrong choice of words. I don't believe you're anyone's girl. You belong entirely to yourself."

"Why that's almost poetic," Emily said, reclaiming her seat. "You surprise me. You surprise me more every day. I'm amazed at the progress you've made. Do you remember my little speech the first time I tried to tutor you? I said something about how a person's manner of speech defines that person. I'll bet you don't remember. You were hopeless."

"Oh yes I remember." An expression, that was almost shyness, came across his face. "You said that 'one cannot aspire to a higher station in life without the ability to express one's self correctly'. Is that right?"

"My goodness! How did you ever remember that?"

"I'll be dam...er...darned if I know. The words just kept running through my mind." He laughed self-consciously.

"That's incredible, she said, "But in all honesty, you have reached that point. Your speech is that of an educated person. How did you do it?"

"Listening to you and reading. I must have read more then forty books over the winter."

"Forty!" she said. "When did you ever find the time?"

"Evenings. Sometimes mornings if I woke up early. It's a joke with my brothers. They say the only way to get my attention is to get between me and the book. And they do that for fun. Stick their heads down in front of the pages."

She laughed. "I'm proud of you. I'm amazed you could do it." She laughed again. "Do you want to know something else?"

He nodded.

"I told your mother it was my belief you didn't have the capacity for learning. She wanted me to prepare you to take over the management of the ranch. I thought it would be impossible. I was honestly convinced of that. Now I'm happy to say I was wrong. You would do fine."

A look of alarm showed on his face. "Oh no. I don't believe I could handle it yet."

"Of course you could. Your mathematics is more than adequate. I doubt that you'd have much application for algebra or geometry here on the ranch. Naturally you should have some exposure to trigonometry and calculus, but you really wouldn't need any of those, either. I never got into higher mathematics in my schooling, so I'm afraid you'd need to dig out that information by yourself. I was trying to learn algebra and geometry along with you, if you recall."

"Wouldn't you want to know trigonometry and calculus for your teaching in case some of your students got that far along?" Andrew didn't want to miss the thrill of continuing to sit with her, head to head, as they pored over text books.

"I suppose so," she said. "But for keeping the ranch accounts, as we've seen, plain old mathematics will do quite nicely. Your mother and brothers have been very helpful in writing down all transactions, so that makes it easy. I'm glad your mother agreed to have that little safe shipped out from Chicago. I was nervous seeing all that money and the important papers kept in a box."

He suddenly stood. "Come on. I want you to take a ride with me."

"What?" she said, surprised. "Why?"

"I'll show you."

"Where?"

"Down by the river."

Emily was reluctant. "What is it?"

"I'll show you."

She giggled. "Big secret, is that right?"

"Yup,"

"Might as well," she said standing. "I'm already dressed for it."


They stood on the bank of the river looking at a lone, tall tree on the other side. "After I'd studied geometry and looked at Pythagoras's theorem, I came down here to see if I could make it work. I put these stakes here in the ground. These two line up on the tree. Then I made use of Pythagoras's theorem—the easy three-four-five right triangle—to lay out this line that I projected along the bank, perpendicular to the other line." Andrew indicated a line of stakes.

"Wait," she said. "You're getting ahead of me."

"I'll show you." He began walking along the river bank motioning for her to follow. "I figured if I could place an identical triangle on this line, laid out like the first one, there'd be one point where the hypotenuse would line up with the tree. That way I'd have created a big right triangle, with the distance to the tree as one side and this line along the bank as another. It's sides would have the same relationship as the small triangle. I measured the length of this side that runs along the bank and compared it to the same side on a small triangle. Then I applied that ratio to the other sides of the large triangle to find the distance to the tree. It's one hundred and eighty-seven feet." He appeared pleased with himself.

Emily looked skeptical. "I'll need to think about that."

"I'll show you on paper when we get back. Knowing the distance to the tree made it easy to determine its height. Sixty-nine feet. These are approximations, of course."

"How do you know you're correct?" she said.

"If you mean did I swim the river and climb the tree to prove it, no I didn't."

She stood for a long period studying the tree and the stakes, shaking her head occasionally.

"There may be an easier way to solve this, but I couldn't think of one," he said. "Are you ready to go back?"

She nodded and walked over to the mare. She wore the same puzzled expression all the way back to the ranch.

# 19

Spring gave way to summer and the children were dismissed from school to enjoy the summer recess. Emily became a full-time resident at the ranch. Not much persuasion was required, since she would be saving the expense of remaining in the boarding house. She began, in earnest, the task of organizing the ranch's paperwork, which she had found in disarray but had no time for it while teaching. There was a great amount of correspondence required to clarify certain matters and some inventive manipulation of records to avoid close scrutiny of ranch property ownership. The teacher suffered pangs of guilt in that endeavor, but rationalized that no harm was being imposed on other people by her actions. What did it matter way out in the wilds of Montana?

"Once we become a state," she told the big man seated beside her at the dining table, "there will be a lot more regulation and controls put into place. We'd better be able to show proper order of our legal documentation."

Andrew had been made a not-totally-willing partner in that undertaking, but accepted any situation that allowed him to spend time with his teacher.

"What a marvelous period of time we are entering." Her eyes shined with enthusiasm. "So many events taking place. Have you heard about a Scotsman, named Bell, back in Boston who has invented a way for people to communicate through a wire?"

"You mean the telegraph? They've done that for years."

"No no!" she said. "They talk. The talking goes through the wire."

He gave her a look of disbelief. "How can they do that?"

"I can't imagine. There must be some way to make the sound change to electricity which goes through the wire like it does with the telegraph."

"It would be interesting to learn how that's done," he said. "I don't understand electricity. Someone told me it's like lightning or what you see when you rub a cat's fur in the dark. They must rub a lot of cats to get the telegraph to work."

"Don't be foolish," she scolded. "I don't have anything on the subject and I'm quite sure there's nothing in any of Henrik's books, but if I write and ask Papa to send me some information, he'd be happy to do it. Of course I'd expect to receive some sarcastic remarks from him along with the material. I've been getting quite enough of that since I sent them the picture." She showed a scornful expression. "He'll ask why a desperado like me needs electricity when I'm so well armed otherwise."

Andrew chuckled. "If it's like lightning, it sure would make Marta run faster."

"Oh you!" She slapped him playfully.

He held up his hands to ward off further abuse. "You're not going to shoot me, are you?"

Emily grinned. "Not today. I've got other things to do, but if you don't behave, I won't write that letter to Papa. Speaking of electricity, Mother wrote and told me that some friends are thinking about installing Mister Edison's electric lights in their homes. Can you imagine?"

Andrew shook his head. "Don't think I want to have any more lightning running around in our house. We had that one time during a real fierce storm. Sort of a bluish glow in the room, sparking here and there." He grinned at the young woman. "They can keep their electricity."

"It's in wires, silly." She became thoughtful. "I'm going to ask Papa to send some law books, also. I know you enjoy reading about law. If you have any dealings with the government, in the future, it's best you be prepared."

"Won't that cost quite a bit? We'd better send him some money."

"Not necessary," she said. "He's a doctor. He can afford it."

"I don't want him to do that," he said, his manner severe. "We can afford it, too. Ask him to send the books, but tell him to let us know the cost so we can pay him back."

Emily yielded. "Of course, if that's what you want." She stood up from the table and stretched. "That's enough for now. I've got to get some air. I think I'll go riding." She looked at her pupil. "Want to come along?"

"Better not," he said. "I've got some work to do on the corral. Some of the boards have been kicked loose. Where are you going?"

"Thought I'd ride east today. I've seen quite a bit of the ranch, but I haven't been out that way. Now that I'm a full-time ranch employee, I'd better lend your brothers a hand and earn my salary."

"Well don't get lost," he cautioned. "Once you lose sight of the ranch buildings, all that country out there looks the same, unless you were born and grew up in it." He stood and began gathering papers. "Of course you can always find your way back by going west toward the setting sun. You'll hit either the trail to town or the river. Then you'll know where you are. Just to be on the safe side, you'd better tie on a bedroll and throw some grub in your saddle bags."

A scowl showed on her pretty face. "I'm not going that far or be gone that long."

"Do it!" he commanded.

It was midmorning before Emily started out over the gently rolling terrain. Several times she looked back to check her position in respect to the ranch until, finally, it was not there. A glance at the sun assured her she was still traveling in an eastward direction. Andrew was correct, she thought looking around. It does all have the same appearance.

Although somewhat apprehensive, she was enjoying the ride. "Good girl, Marta," she said patting the mare's neck. "You'll take care of me, won't you? You could probably find your way home even if I couldn't."

When her stomach told her it was something past noon, she pulled a small loaf of bread and some sliced roast beef from her saddle bag. As Marta continued along, she gnawed with satisfaction on the bread and meat.

They passed scattered herds of the longhorn cattle, usually gathered near small streams. Emily caught sight of the JK brand and decided she was still on ranch property. Then she saw smoke on the other side of a little rise. Who could be out here, she wondered. Curious, she turned the mare toward the rise. On the other side she saw two men standing near the fire among a small herd of cattle. Several calves were on the ground. Approaching, she recognized Franklin and Zachary at the same time they saw her.

"Well now, gal," the younger Jones brother said, "what brings you out this-a-way? Are you lost?"

"Nope," she answered, falling into a now familiar lingo. "Thought I'd mosey on over and plug me a couple of rustlers."

The two laughed. "I wouldn't doubt it," Zachary said. "You look ready for us," he said pointing to the revolver strapped to her hip.

She grinned and climbed down from the horse. "Found some that weren't branded, did you?"

"Four bulls and a couple of heifers." Zachary pulled a piece of paper from his shirt pocket and handed it to the young woman. "Already branded the heifers. Wrote 'em down, too."

Emily looked at the four calves on the ground, each with three legs tied together. Some bawled and tried to stand. Several anxious mothers hovered nearby. They bellowed and swung their long horns in a threatening manner. As the woman eyed the cows cautiously, Franklin yelled and waved his hat until they retreated a few yards.

"'Bout ready to give this bull the treatment," the younger brother said. "Want to watch?"

"Treatment?" she said hesitantly.

"If you'll notice, with the bulls we tie the two front legs to one back leg. That's so we can spread the back legs," he said with a devilish grin."

"Oh, I see," she said, blushing as she realized the significance of his remark.

"Come here, so you can see what I'm doin'."

Repulsed, but on the other hand morbidly intrigued, she edged closer and watched as he made the cut and removed the small globules of flesh. The little animal bawled piteously and Emily almost lost her lunch.

Franklin pulled a pouch from his pocket and poured a small amount of the contents in his hand.

"What's that?" she said.

"Salt. Don't know how much good it does but we ain't never had any get infected so we keep on usin' it." He emptied his hand into the open cut he'd made in the calf. Then he rolled the animal over so its right side was exposed. Zachary approached with the branding iron and the young woman was subjected to the sight and smell of a branding at close range. "We always brand on the right side," he told her. "Makes it easier to spot.

"That's it," Franklin said as he pulled loose the tie on the calf's legs.

Emily watched the little animal scramble up and run away, on tottery legs, toward its mother. "It's so cruel," she mumbled, instantly embarrassed that the words had escaped her.

"Yup." the number three brother said. "Life ain't easy for cattle, 'specially the steers. They get branded and cut, have to make it through cold winters, hot summers and hungry wolves, don't get enough to eat at times, get driven over eighty miles to the railroad, crammed into cattle cars to be carried to Chicago for slaughterin' and to fill somebuddy's belly." He grinned at the woman. "But then, that's the way it is. Next one's yours." He pointed to another young bull.

"Oh no!" Emily said, shuddering.

He gave her a long look. "You have to do it if you're going to know all about life on a cattle ranch. Or would you just rather know about the nice parts?"

"I'll show you," he said rolling another young bull on its back.

"No! No!" she said and, after a long moment's hesitation, in almost a whisper, "yes."

He handed her the knife and told her to straddle the calf. Holding the legs separated, he showed her where to cut. "Just a little slit," he said. "Don't need to be very big."

With the calf bawling and perspiration pouring off her face, Emily gritted her teeth and made the cut.

"Now just squeeze there. That's it. And out it comes. Take hold and cut it off. Atta' girl. Now here's some salt."

When she finished, the young schoolteacher was white and shaking.

"Not done yet," he told her, rolling the calf on its side. "Hand her the branding iron, Zach. Now put it here on the upper hip while you count to three."

Emily could barely stand as she watched the released calf run away. She looked at the blood on her fingers and thought she'd be sick. In spite of her abhorrence of the act she had performed, the young woman felt a strange satisfaction.

As she rode back to the ranch that evening, in the company of the two Jones brothers, she knew she had undergone another experience that she would not mention to her parents.

# 20

Fall was approaching and Emily knew that in a few weeks school would begin again. During the summer she had divided her time at the ranch house between organizing the paperwork and providing instruction to her pupil in disciplines where her knowledge was still superior to his. In English and literature she still held an edge, but with mathematics, Andrew had gone well beyond the point where she could provide assistance. The law books, sent by her father, he read voraciously. Emily was amazed by his quick assimilation of the subject. His law study brought about an acute interest in history and geography, particularly as related to law. Their after-dinner discussions were both long and intense, which caused the table to be vacated by the other brothers in short order. Karen Jones usually sat listening—once in a while allowing a smile of satisfaction to show.

On those days when the big man was busy with a building or repairing project and her records had been brought up to date, Emily would be found out on the range with the older brothers. Escorted by one or another of the Jones men, she gradually became acquainted with the spread. Patrolling the boundaries, they turned back cattle from adjoining ranches and moved the Jones cattle back further onto the ranch property.

Those without brands and uncastrated bulls, mostly young stock, were dealt with on the

spot.    William   and   Zachary,   being   more
chivalrous, spared the young woman those parts
of  the  chore  she  found  most  distasteful,  but
Franklin, with fiendish delight, insisted she tend
to every other animal.

With   tutelage,   provided   by   William,   she
became  fairly  accomplished  with  the  lariat.   She
attempted the craft with young stock only.

"Catch  one  of  them  bigger  bulls,  it  could
drag  that  little  mare  you're  ridin'  all  over  the
range," the Jones man had said.

She had no success in learning to rope the
back legs of an animal as she'd seen Franklin do
during the roundup.

"Frank is one of the best," William told her
by  way  of  consolation.   "None  I  know  can  do
better."


"You're  late."    The  two  brothers  were
hitching  teams  of  horses  to  another  cattle  shed,
that had been completed, preparing to drag it out
on  the  range.    Both  smiled  their  greetings  as
Emily, dressed in her riding clothes, approached.
"Billy and Zach left early," Franklin added.

"Your  mother  is  going  to  town  today,"  she
said.  "I wanted to finish a letter for her to mail."

"I  can't  ride  with  you  today.   Gotta  help
Puddin...oops...I mean Andy with this shed."

The  teacher  had,  on  numerous  occasions,
expressed her displeasure with the nickname that
the  other  brothers  applied  to  her  pupil.   "That's
fine." she told them.  "I know my way around by
now.  I can ride alone."

Andrew  showed  a  worried  frown.   "I  don't
think  that's  a  good  idea.   Something  could

happen."

"Nothing is going to happen." She was somewhat irritated with him being overly protective of her. "I can take care of myself. Where did William and Zachary go?"

"Northeast," she was told.

"Then I'll go southeast toward Cuthbertson's place. We haven't been out that way for a while."

Andrew's grin hid his concern. "Now don't you get too cozy with that feller. Remember what I told you about him?"

Her lips tightened. "I have no intention of seeing Mister Cuthbertson, so that shouldn't be a problem."

"Why don't you wait until tomorrow?" The younger Jones brother was clearly apprehensive. "Then Frank can ride with you."

"Oh you!" The Irish temper flared. "You're starting to treat me like a baby. I'm going alone."

Andrew shrugged. "All right, but take along some grub. You still have a bedroll tied on your saddle, don't you?"

"Yes, even though I don't understand why you insist I carry it. I'll be back before dark."

Franklin chuckled. "That's one of Ma's rules—not Andy's. We usually don't pay much attention to it, except for Billy. As you know, he rides alone most of the time. Once in a while he runs out of daylight when he's way out on the east side, so he camps out. I don't cotton to sleepin' on the ground, myself, but that's Billy."

The teacher's curiosity had been aroused. "Why did your mother make that rule?"

Franklin ignored his younger brother's look of warning. "Andy's never told you? Probably doesn't want to worry you, but it happened years ago. Ma was out riding alone one winter when her horse fell and broke a leg. She was quite a ways out and knew she couldn't walk in before dark. She didn't have a bedroll with her, so she snuggled up to the horse to stay warm. Pa and Henny rode all night lookin' for her. Didn't find her until daylight. By then she'd finished off the horse and started walking."

"She killed the horse?"

"Sure." Franklin shrugged. "That's all you can do for a horse with a broken leg. After that she never went out on the range without food and a bedroll. Tried to make the rest of us do it too. We usually don't unless we're workin' way out."

Andrew had been pacing, with hands jammed in his pockets, while his brother talked. Then he turned to his teacher. "You're probably right—nothing is going to happen—but it doesn't cost you anything to be careful."

In the early afternoon she came upon a herd of cattle in a swale where a small stream flowed. Spotting an unbranded heifer calf, she put a tie cord in her teeth and shook out her lariat. She caught the calf on her third try. As the mare held tension on the rope, her rider jumped to the ground. The little animal, caught in the noose, tried to dodge as Emily approached, but she grabbed the rope with one gloved hand. From the calf's side, she reached across its back, and snatched a front and back leg. In lifting the calf, she lost her balance and sat down with the animal upside down on her lap. The two regarded each other for a moment.

Emily sighed in exasperation and added another leg to the two she held and tied the three.

"Well Marta," she said to the mare. "What do you think of this? You're not going to tell anyone what you've just seen, are you?"

As the calf began bawling and struggling on top of the woman, its mother boldly approached, answering its offspring's cries with bellows of rage. Emily threw her hat at the cow that was waving its horns threateningly close. It retreated a few yards, then began jabbing a horn into the hat.

"Hey!" the woman shouted. "Stop that!" She drew her pistol and placed a shot next to the hat.

With rocks and dirt showering her face, and startled by the loud explosion from the gun, the cow quickly gave up the argument and ran away.

Emily squirmed from under the calf, losing a boot in the process. She was relieved to find her hat had not been pierced by the horn. That would require some explanation back at the ranch, she thought, pulling on her boot. After dusting off and replacing her hat, she set about making a fire.

With the calf branded and released, she cooled the branding iron in the stream, coiled her lariat and remounted Marta. Passing near the herd, she noticed an unfamiliar brand—a simple C. "Cuthbertson," she said aloud. What should I do? she thought. Should I just let it go and tell the Jones family or run it back toward his place?

"No!" she told the mare. "I'm not going to let that reprobate feed his stock on our grass." 'Our grass'? She was shocked by the realization of her sudden proprietary concern for ranch property. "Jones' grass," she corrected herself.

Having decided, she cut the heifer from the herd and started the animal back toward the

Cuthbertson ranch. Maybe he's intentionally letting his heifers go onto the Jones ranch to have them bred by Hereford bulls. Probably doesn't have one himself. She examined that thought as she rode along.

It was shortly after she crossed, what she assumed to be, the boundary between the Jones and Cuthbertson properties that she spotted the rider. She knew she'd been seen when he turned his horse in her direction. Might be the scoundrel himself, she thought. She considered turning immediately and riding away but decided she must explain the heifer.

"I heard a shot," he said drawing near. "Thought I'd better take a look."

She recognized Cuthbertson from seeing him in town. "That was me," she told him. "Shot at a rattler." She wasn't going to admit having to shoo a cow away while she lay under its calf.

Emily was recognized also. "You're that schoolmarm that's stayin' out at the Jones place. Almost didn't know you in them duds.

"I brought your heifer back. It was with some of our cattle." There I go again, she thought. Saying "our".

"What are you doin' herdin' cattle?" he wanted to know. "That ain't hardly a lady's job— 'specially a schoolteacher lady."

Reluctantly she provided an answer. "The ranch is short-handed. Thought I'd help out this summer." She turned the mare to ride away.

"Whoa!" he said. "Hold on a minute. Maybe you'd like to come by the shack for some coffee?"

Emily turned in the saddle to answer. "No thank you. I've got to get back to work." Sometime later, when she looked back again, she saw he was following her. She stopped and turned the mare. "What is it, Mister Cuthbertson?"

"Nothin'," he said. "Just thought I'd ride along to keep you company for a while."

"That won't be necessary," she said. She felt her heart begin pounding.

"Now that's not very neighborly. We ought to get better acquainted."

"That won't be possible." In spite of her shallow breathing, she managed to keep her voice calm. "I think you should just take your cow and leave."

"Why now, I wouldn't want to do that." He was showing her a leer. "Tain't often I get a chance to keep company with a lady purdy as you. Bet you're really somethin' under that cowboy getup." He rode close and reached for the mare's reins.

She jerked the horse's head away from his reach and pulled her pistol. "Mister Cuthbertson!" she said through clinched teeth, "do you want me to shoot you?"

"Now wait a minute," he said holding up his free hand. He took note of the fact that the weapon was pointed at the center of his chest. "Why would you want to do somethin' like that?"

"Because you're trespassing on Jones land and I don't believe your intentions toward me are of the highest order. You're not going to make use of me like you did with that young Adams girl."

His face darkened. "How do you know about that?"

"Everyone knows about that. Now ride off."

He began backing his horse until he was some distance away. "I'll bet you can't hit the broad side of a barn with that thing. All I have to do is let you get out of pistol range and then I'll take down your horse with this." He slapped the rifle strapped to his saddle.

As they sat staring at each other, a rage grew within her, brought about by his threat to shoot her beloved Marta. Out of the corner of her eye she caught sight of a crow that landed on a bush to her right. She swung the pistol and fired. Cuthbertson's jaw and the crow dropped simultaneously. He stared alternately at the dead bird and the young woman, her gun brought to bear on his chest again. She came forward—her face grim. When she spoke, her voice held a deadly edge. "Compared to that crow, Mister Cuthbertson, you make a mighty big target. Now I want you to throw down your pistol and rifle."

"Like hell I will." He managed a tight grin. "I don't think a nice lady like you would shoot a man down in cold blood."

"Very well, Mister Cuthbertson." Her voice was almost a whisper. "I'm not going to kill you, but I'm going to make sure you can't use those weapons. You're right handed so that's the arm I'm going to shoot. You should be able to make it to town to get treatment unless I hit an artery and you bleed to death. Now hold steady. If you move I might hit something vital."

He saw the barrel of the gun align with his right arm. "W...wait a m...min...minute, Miss," he pleaded, shifting his arm behind his back.

"That won't help," she said. "Now I'll have to shoot you in the shoulder." The gun lifted slightly.

"M...Miss. P...p...please don't." His chin quivered and perspiration trickled down his face. "I'll d...drop m...my guns."

Emily seemed reluctant to give that new development any consideration, but finally relented. "Very well, Mister Cuthbertson, but do it very carefully. Unbuckle your gun belt and let it fall."

The man was quick to comply.

"Now turn your horse so I can see your rifle. Take your knife and cut the straps that hold the scabbard. Don't touch the gun or you'll lose an arm." When the rifle was on the ground she told him to go and never approach her again. Then added, "If I see any more of your stock on Jones land, I'll shoot them."

He was several hundred yards away when he turned and shouted, "you haven't heard the last of me! You'll pay for this!"

Emily was still suffering bouts of un- controllable trembling when she reached the ranch. The brothers saw the rifle she held and the gun belt hanging on the saddle horn. "What happened?" Andrew said taking the rifle.

She dismounted and rushed into the house before the brothers could see her tears. It was dinner time before she had collected herself so she could tell the story.

# 21

THE WAGON SPOKE
THE VOICE OF BROKEN WAGON & VICINITY
AUG. 24, 1889 5 CENTS PROP: MARVIN T. JENSEN

It is being reported in our community that a rancher east of town was disarmed at gunpoint by a certain lady school-teacher when he made unwelcome advances of the type which may have been visited upon several other young ladies in the area. The guns have been returned and their owner properly reprimanded for behavior unbecoming a gentleman.

It appears to all that his health has been deteriorating since the above mentioned event occurred and he has been encouraged to seek a more moderate climate. A request has been made that the citizens of Broken Wagon and elsewhere be notified of an auction to be held at his ranch on Saturday next, to dispose of his property prior to an impending move.

Emily's face burned as she stood on the walkway in front of Hansen's Mercantile, reading the latest issue of the town paper. She had moved back into her old room at Missus Larson's boarding house the day after the noted event took place. That was three days ago. School was scheduled to start the following Monday and she had preparations to make.

Folks passing by gave her friendly smiles. It didn't help—she was having difficulty holding back tears.

"Now you're a hero."

She started at the sound of his voice behind her and whirled around. "Franklin! What are you doing in town?"

"Pickin' up some supplies." He grinned. "I see you got the word."

"You've seen this," she said holding out the paper.

"Heard about it." He saw the pools forming in her eyes.

"Oh Franklin!" she wailed. "This is terrible. If my parents ever hear about this I'll never be able to face them."

"There there," he said taking hold and patting her hand. "It's not that bad. You did this town a big favor."

"But I look like a fool. I don't know how I can get up in front of a class."

"They'll be happy to see you. Like I said, now you're a hero."

She let a small smile show. "I'd rather not be that type of hero." She held up the paper again. "What does this mean—that he was properly reprimanded?"

"Oh!" he said laughing. "That was ol' Pud...Andy. The day you came into town, he took off with Cuthbertson's guns. Said he was goin' to have a talk with Noel. I have a hunch Noel didn't offer much to the conversation. Andy came back with skinned knuckles. Sometimes his language is a little rough."

"Oh my goodness! I saw Cuthbertson yesterday," she said thoughtfully. "When he saw me, he crossed the street. He looked awful with bumps and bruises all over his face. And he walked hunched over like an old man."

"Trouble with his ribs, I reckon. Andy was a mite riled." If Franklin meant to show sympathy, he failed.

"He shouldn't have done that. He might have seriously injured the man."

A harsh laugh burst from the Jones brother. "Now that's one for the books. It's just possible a gunshot would have injured him too. You were ready to shoot him, weren't you?"

"No!" she answered quickly. "I don't believe I would have shot him." She grinned. "He didn't know that, however. I'm almost sorry for his humiliation and the thrashing he took. I hope he's not hurt too badly."

"Noel will be all right. He's purdy tough."

"Is he really leaving?" She gave him a questioning look. "It says in this paper he's having an auction on Saturday."

"That's what I hear. I'll be goin' out there with Ma. His property borders on ours, so she wants it. Cattle and all."

Emily looked at the brother with serious eyes. "It doesn't seem proper that she'd be taking advantage of his situation."

Franklin grinned at the young woman who could still feel sorry for someone who had threatened her with harm. "Don't worry about that," he said. "Ma will give him more than a fair price with the understanding that he never shows his face again in Montana."

"More land and more cattle," Emily said. "Will she ever have enough?"

"I doubt it," he said chuckling. "And it looks like you're going to have more paperwork to take care of."

"That's all I need," she said.


Franklin had been correct. When she stood in front of her class to start the school year, the youngsters regarded her with awe. Even Frida was polite, but she couldn't help saying, "Miss O'Neill, did you really scare Mister Cuthbertson into leaving the territory?"

"Now Frida," the teacher answered, "this is not going to be a topic for discussion."

"Oh Miss O'Neill!" the child cried, her eyes wide with wonder, "when I grow up I want to be just like you and carry a pistol."

"No you don't, Frida," Emily said. "I carried the gun for protection when I was working on the Jones ranch this summer. As you've heard, I was attacked by an Indian with a knife last fall. Andrew Jones came to my rescue." The teacher couldn't resist embellishing the story for the children's entertainment. "After that I felt it prudent to be armed. I didn't carry the gun because it was something I wanted. I thought it necessary."

I shouldn't lie to the children, she silently chastised herself. To tell the truth, I enjoyed carrying the weapon. It gave me a feeling of power.

"All right class, ..." she began, but Frida couldn't be stilled.

"Miss O'Neill, did you like wearing cowboy clothes?"

As she considered an answer, Emily

wondered how long she should allow the conversation to continue. She had to admit to herself she was having a good time responding to the child's curiosity. "Well, Frida, it's like I was told, it's just not practical to try wearing a long dress and sit astride a horse herding cattle. There are, as you know, sidesaddles that allow a woman, in a long skirt, to sit with both legs on one side of the horse, but out there on the range, doing the work I was doing, she wouldn't be sitting long." She smiled as the girl, along with the rest of the class, laughed knowingly.

And yet someone had to say, "why not?"

In response, the teacher said, "How many of you have herded cattle on a well-trained cow pony?"

Hans, Tom and several other boys raised their hands.

"Well, then you know these horses can turn very fast trying to head-off a heifer or steer. I had to learn the hard way." She winked and rubbed her backside to the delight of the class. "And I was astraddle the horse," she added. "I had several falls and several near falls this past summer. If I'd been riding sidesaddle, I would have been on the ground most of the time."

The class laughed and giggled their approval. The next question came from eight-year-old Judith. "Why did you want to be a cowboy...," she looked around shyly at her laughing classmates, "...or is it cowgirl?"

Emily laughed along with the children. "I didn't think I wanted to be a cowgirl, Judith, but I've been working for the Jones family for almost a year. It began when they needed help for a roundup last fall. Hans and Tom were there. I guess I thought it would be fun. An adventure. It turned out to be dirty, hard and dangerous work. And do you know what?" She grinned at her pupils. "Now don't tell your mothers, but I loved every minute of it."

When the laughter died, Hans yelled from the back of the room, "even when you was caught in the stampede?"

The teacher put on a wry face. "Well..."

"Oh please, Missus O'Neill," several children called out. "Please tell us about it."

So for the rest of the morning, the class was held spellbound by tales of their cowgirl teacher's adventures.

# 22

Emily had called another of her occasional meetings to apprise the Jones family of the current status of the ranch business. In the early October afternoon they sat around the dinner table while the teacher gave her report. Only William was absent.

"Where is he, anyway?" the teacher wanted to know.

Franklin answered, frowning. "Said he was goin' to check on things out toward the east side. Be back for dinner."

"He's not usually on time for nothin," the older brother said. "Reckon he'll be along in a bit." He grinned at the others. "Don't think he'll mind missin' this powwow."

Emily shrugged. "I think we did quite well with the sale. At least we had more than one buyer show up at the railroad yards." She smiled with self satisfaction. The letter I sent to the Chicago Board of Trade did some good, she thought. "The five-hundred and sixty head of Jones steers, with the Hereford strain, brought the best prices. Cuthbertson's eighty-seven longhorn steers sold for something less than they would have last year. The buyers wanted steers with more Hereford in them. Said the sooner we bred the longhorn out of our cattle the more we'd prosper."

The teacher's face registered consternation. There I go again. Using "we" and "our". I've got to stop doing that. A quick glance at Karen Jones showed, by the older woman's slight smile, that she'd caught the slip.

"Total received on the sale was ten-thousand, four-hundred and seventy-seven dollars. Add five-hundred, thirty for the lumber sold to Mister Ronstat for his store and subtract the fifty-eight hundred to buy out Cuthbertson, and we have a net...," damn it, she thought, I did it again,"... of five-thousand, two-hundred and seven dollars." She barely stopped herself from asking if there was any questions. This isn't the classroom, she told herself.

"The herd," she began, careful not to imply any suggestion of possessiveness, "should number about two-thousand, eighteen, taking into account Cutherbertson.s bunch, the steers sold, those lost and the calves born since the count." She decided not to mention the amount of cash on hand, aware that the Jones mother was rather sensitive about having that knowledge dispensed. Wonder why she trusts me knowing about it?

"That's it," she finished.

Karen Jones nodded with a smile.

The brothers stood and stretched. Franklin pulled out his pocket watch. "Wonder what's keepin' Billy...William," he corrected himself with a quick glance at his mother. "Reckon I'll take a ride out and see what's holdin' 'im up."

"I'll come along," Emily said.


"You think we'll make it then?" Franklin gave her a quizzical look as they rode over the gently rolling terrain. Patches of snow still remained from an early storm.

"What can stop you," Emily said, shivering in her sheepskin-lined coat, "as long as beef prices hold?"

"They'll hold," he said. "Why hell," he added, "more and more people keep comin' into America from ever' place on earth and they've got to eat." He grinned at her. "All those Irishmen have flooded the country since the potato famine."

"Oh you!" she said, swinging her rope at him. "What about those Norwegians and English.

"They probably came first. The English, anyway. And Jones is an English name."

He ducked, laughing, as she swung the rope again. "I don't rightly know what breed Pa was. A little of everthin', he always said. I reckon an Englishman got into the picture somehow."

"From knowing Andrew and hearing about your father, he must have been a big Englishman."

The Jones brother pulled off his hat and scratched his head vigorously. "Can't help you there. Could have been a gorilla swingin' in the family tree for all I know."

"Silly!" She appeared to study the man riding next to her. "Yes," she said at length. "I can see the resemblance—the prominent lower jaw, the recessed forehead, sunken eyes. Now if you had more hair I'd know for sure."

He sat grinning at the charming, young woman and wondering if he would have a chance with her. Probably not, he decided. And I'm sure not going to try making any moves on her while she's carrying that pistol, he thought. Not after what happened to Noel. Besides, Ma would kill me.

"Billy's probably out in this area," he said with a sweep of his arm. "With winter comin', he

154

wanted to move the herds a little closer to the ranch so we wouldn't hafta haul hay so far. We'll cover more ground if we split up. You head on over that-a-way for about a half mile. I'll go this way. If you find him, fire a couple shots. I'll do the same." He turned his horse and rode away.

It was almost a half hour later that she heard gunfire. She turned the mare and galloped toward the sound. A few minutes passed and then more shots. She adjusted her direction. When she came upon the scene, her heart almost stopped. William was lying on the ground with his head held by his sobbing, older brother. A dead cow lay nearby as did a bawling calf with its legs tied. "What happened?" she said, jumping down from the mare, although it was obvious.

William's shirt was soaked with blood. He turned his head weakly at the sound of her voice and showed a small smile. "Got careless. Turned my back on 'er." He nodded toward the cow. "She got me in the back. Had to shoot 'er." His pistol lay on the ground next to his hand.

"Quick!" she commanded. "Take off his shirt!" She removed the bedroll from her saddle, took out the thinner blanket and began tearing it into strips.

Franklin stared at the young woman, dumbly, tears on his face.

"Now!" she yelled. "Get the shirt off, now! Cut it off! Tear it off! Do it!"

Franklin was jolted into action. He ripped open the shirt front, pulled it from the trousers and slipped it off his brother's back.

"Now pull the underwear down to his waist." With the strips of blanket material in her hands, she knelt next to the men. "Turn him over. I want to see."

The older brother did as instructed.

Emily winced seeing the large puncture wound just under the ribs, still flowing blood. "Hold him up. I've got to wrap this cloth around him as tight as I can to slow the bleeding."

Franklin looked at the woman as, with clenched teeth, she began wrapping the wound. William groaned. "Are you sure you know what you're doin'? You're hurtin' him."

"My father's a doctor. I've been helping him since I was a girl." She pulled the fabric tighter. "Of course I'm hurting him, but it needs to be done."

She finished the binding and tied the loose end. "Take your knife and cut away that bloody cloth so he doesn't get a chill from it. Quickly! We've got to get some blankets around him so he doesn't get any colder."

Franklin cut away the upper part of his brother's underwear while the young woman retrieved the rest of her bedroll.

"Let's get him up on your horse before we wrap him in the blankets," she said. "You'll need to ride behind to hold him on the saddle."

With great effort, the two managed to lift the wounded man onto the saddle and wrap him in blankets. When Franklin was seated behind his brother, he asked, "what are you goin' to do?"

"I'm taking William's horse and ride for help. He's bigger and faster than Marta."

"He's also more of a handful." His look was doubtful. "Think you can handle 'im?"

"I'll handle him." she said. "Get going!" As they started off, she quickly removed the lariat and the tie on the calf's legs so it could run free. Afterward she put William's gun and Marta's bridle in her saddlebag and started the mare toward the ranch. William's big horse shied away as the strange woman approached. She managed to grab a rein. "Whoa, damn you!" she shouted. Pulling the horse's head close, she looked him in the eye. "Behave, you son of a bitch, or I'll shoot you dead."

Her manner reminded him of another woman he had carried on occasion, and he knew better than to offer resistance as she climbed on, cast off the lariat and headed him toward the ranch.

As she raced past the brothers, she heard Franklin yell, "Go girl!"


They heard the pistol shots as the rider came into view. "That's Billy's horse, but who's ridin' it like that?" Zachary stood squinting.

Andrew had seen that figure before. "That's Emily. Something's happened."

She was yelling even as the horse stormed into the yard, lathered and winded. "William is hurt! Franklin is bringing him." She leaped from the horse. "Zachary, get the buckboard and go after the doctor." Then she turned to the other brother. "Andrew, we've got to take the wagon and go back after him. I'll get some more blankets. He's got to be kept warm."

It never occurred to the brothers to question their orders. Both ran to hitch up their respective teams. Emily met Karen Jones on the porch. She stopped to explain, but the older woman waved her inside. "Jeg hørte. Gå!" Then the older woman yelled, "Hagen!"

Hagen was leading the spent horse away as Emily emerged from the house with arms full of blankets. Those she carried to the covered wagon and threw inside. She heard Missus Jones say to the boy, in Norwegian, to put a blanket on the horse and walk him until he was cool.

In short order the men had the harnessed teams hitched and ready to go. Emily was already on the seat to be with the driver. The Jones woman crawled into the back of the wagon.

"We'll meet you along the road," the teacher called out to Zachary as he climbed on the buckboard and started the team.

Andrew seated himself and took up the reins.

"That way," the young woman pointed.

# 23

"Is Billy goin' to be all right?" Hans Vik said even before he'd taken his seat in the classroom.

The teacher smiled at the youth for his concern. She knew how much he admired the Jones brother, with whom he had worked during the roundup. "He's in bad shape—lost a lot of blood—but doctor Morrison said he should pull through unless a bad infection sets in."

"When will he know?"

"It might be a week or two before he's certain. I told the doctor that if he needs any advice, my father would consult with a number of prominent doctors in New York who could offer help. Doctor Morrison composed a telegram that I sent to my father. We should be getting an answer in a day or two."

"Isn't your father a doctor?"

"Yes Frida, he is." Emily knew she could always depend on the eleven year old to jump with both feet into any conversation.

"Then why does he hafta con...cons...?"

"Consult, it means to ask another for information," the teacher provided.

"Why does he hafta consult with other doctors?"

"No one doctor knows everything, Frida. The body is very complex. Some doctors have had experience treating certain problems that other doctors don't know about. We want the best treatment we can get for William."

Hans spoke again. "I heard doctor Morrison tell Pa that if you hadn't done what you done, William would be dead."

"I remembered a few things working with my father. I guess it's fortunate I remembered some of the correct things. Now then, class, lets get on with our lessons. First, however, I'd like to talk about a very important event that's going to take place in a very short time. Anyone remember what that might be?" The teacher looked out over fifteen faces wearing blank expressions. "Surely you haven't forgotten? We talked about it last spring."

One hand emerged timidly from the group. "Yes Betsy."

"Is it about Montana being a state?"

"Very good, Betsy. In just a few weeks they'll decide, back there in the nation's Capital, whether Montana and three other states will be admitted to the Union. Who remembers the names of those other states? Hans?"

"The Dakotas."

"That's correct, Hans. North and South— our neighbors to the east. And the other?" The teacher scanned the room. "Doesn't anyone remember? Yes Mary."

Mary Winslip looked cautiously around at her classmates before venturing her answer. "Is it Washington?"

"That's very good, Mary. How did you remember?"

The youngster smiled with satisfaction. "I have an uncle in Seattle."

"So there you have it." Emily smiled at her students. "Four states will be added to the Union, and by sometime next year there may be two more—Idaho and Wyoming. How will being a state change Montana?"

Hans was the first to answer. "Pa says we'll hafta start payin' taxes. He don't like that."

"Your father is most likely correct. At present we have a territorial governor. Since all laws and their enforcement are the responsibility of the Federal government, he doesn't have much authority. As a state, Montana will have its own government including a congress, executive and judicial branches. We'll be almost like a separate country. A large number of people will have jobs, working for the state government, and they will need to be paid. Right now, the two major industries in Montana are mining and beef production, so that will be the state's source of money to pay these people."

She looked at Hans and smiled. "I suppose it will be necessary for your father to accept paying taxes as the price of living in a separate country. Frida?"

"Who are those people that will be working in the government?"

Emily smiled. The girl's inquisitiveness was a often a delight to her teacher, although at other times her brash behavior proved annoying. "Any citizen of Montana can be, or grow up to be, an employee of the government. Congressmen will be elected by voters—adult men." She braced herself for the obvious next question from the youngster.

"Why just men?"

"At present, only men in the United States, enjoy the privilege of voting. A number of women are trying to bring about change."

"Would you want to vote?" Frida showed a pixie grin.

"Of course I would." The discussion was

touching on a subject that raised strong feelings in the teacher. "I feel women have as much right to vote as men. I can't understand the rigid position taken on this matter by the leaders of our government." She decided it would be prudent to climb down off her soapbox before she became more agitated.

Frida wasn't finished. "Can my father vote?"

"He can, if he chooses."

"Who will he vote for?" the youngster persisted.

"I expect he'll want to vote for the man to be the congressman from this area, who is best qualified to represent the people here. Of course the citizens would be best served by someone who knew law."

"Would that be Puddin..., would that be Andrew Jones?" the girl said with a sly grin. "Pa heard that Andrew was reading about law and said he didn't know Andrew had enough sense to pour piss out of a boot."

"Freeeida!"

The girl ducked her head to hide her grin as the class burst into laughter.

"I'm going to talk with your parents about the kind of language you're bringing into this classroom." Emily showed the youngster her most stern look, although she could barely manage to hold it.

"Well that's what he said."

"I don't care what he said. I won't allow that sort of talk in school." For emphasis, the teacher moved to stand over the girl.

Frida tried to appear chastised, but the grin kept showing on her face as she sneaked a look at Mary.

Emily returned to the head of the class. "Now then, are there any other questions?"

"Are you still teaching Mister Jones," Betsy said.

Anything that goes on in this town, seems to be everyone's business, the teacher thought. "No, Betsy. There's not much more I can teach him. Besides reading law books, he's teaching himself geometry and trigonometry. I never had those studies in my school, so I can't help him."

"What's geometry and trigonometry?" Hans Vik wanted to know.

Emily stepped to the blackboard and picked up a piece of chalk. "Geometry is a branch of mathematics that defines the ways that shapes and angles can be determined and measured. Trigonometry is a more specific form of geometry having to do with the triangle. Here's a problem Mister Jones showed me." She drew some lines on the board. "This is a wide river and this is a tree on one side. And this is you standing on the other side."

In the afternoon she was standing over Melba, helping the girl with a reading assignment, when the door opened behind her. She turned to look at a man, dressed in a fashion she would have expected to see in New York, but certainly not in Montana. Emily knew she had never seen him before, and yet there was something about him that was vaguely familiar.

"Miss O'Neill," he said. "My name is Henrik Jones."

# 24

"I'm first mate on the steamship Alexandria," Henrik said to the teacher.

They sat in the back of the empty schoolroom talking. Emily had used the excuse of an approaching storm to dismiss the children early.

"The ship is laid up in a Seattle dry dock for repairs. We hit a bad storm that did a lot of damage. Thought I'd use the time to visit the family." He scowled. "After seeing Billy, I'm glad I did."

He's an extremely handsome man, the teacher thought—a tall, well-built, blond man with a strong face and good features like his mother—and the same blue eyes. Dressed, as he was, with a vest and jacket over a white, ruffled shirt and brown riding trousers tucked into Wellington boots, he presented a dashing figure.

"I have no doubt that William was pleased you came. How did you get here, Mister Jones?"

"Please, Miss O'Neill," he said. "Call me Henrik. My brothers call me Henny."

"I'll do that, Henrik, but then I'm Emily. Your brothers call me Emily."

He laughed, showing strong, white teeth. "Well, I guess they would, Emily. Billy tells me you're part of the family—like a sister. If I'm going to have a sister, I'm glad it's a beautiful young woman like you, Emily O'Neill. Now, back to your question, I caught the Northern Pacific railroad from Seattle to Billings, rented a rig and drove on up. I can't believe how the place has grown in four years. The first folks I saw in town, that I knew, told me about Billy. I went directly over to the doctor's office to see him." Henrik's face showed anxiety. "He looks bad. Do you think he'll pull through?"

"The doctor says he has a good chance. He's young and strong. The only problem might be infection." Emily wanted to ease his concern. "My father is a doctor back in New York. He's consulting with other doctors to determine the best treatment. Doctor Morrison is waiting for the information."

"I appreciate what you're doing. I talked with Billy for a while, until the doctor kicked me out. He told me you saved his life."

The young woman frowned. "I suppose only time will tell. I pray that I did. For a number of years, my father encouraged me to assist him in treating some patients, so I'm accustomed to seeing wounded people and knowing what he would do under certain conditions." A small smile showed. "At the time I was born, he was hoping for a son who would follow in his footsteps. He got me instead. If he'd thought I would be accepted into a medical school, he would've pushed me in that direction, but I really wanted to be a teacher."

"I would imagine you could be anything you wanted," he said with a smile. "But why did you want to be a teacher way out here in the Montana Territory? It's a long way from New York."

The teacher smiled and shook her head. "I wonder myself. I suppose it was an opportunity to experience an entirely different way of living. It certainly has been that."

"Do you expect to stay on?"

"Oh no." A slight frown appeared on her face. "I'll be here for the remainder of this school year, but after that..."

"I know what you mean," he said. "This isn't New York, or even San Francisco. Hardly a place for a city girl."

Emily bristled. "I wouldn't say that. This city girl has done all right."

"Of course," he said hurriedly. "I didn't mean you couldn't deal with it. It's quite a change. I just don't think you'd want to."

"I'm not sure. There are times I wonder what in the world am I doing here. Other times I wonder what I'd be doing anywhere else." As Emily looked around the classroom, her face softened. "The children. I love the children."

"I'll bet the feeling is mutual." The Jones brother grinned at the young woman. "While I was sitting back here waiting, I couldn't help but notice the affection they have for you. I'll wager you're a wonderful teacher."

She gave him a shy grin. "I hope so. It's so much more difficult having a class with such a wide range of ages. A real challenge."

"Seems like you have all the answers, but say...," Henrik pulled the watch from his fob pocket, "...I'd better leave if I'm going to make it out to the ranch this evening."

"No!" she said, rising to look out the door. "You can't do that. It's going to be raining, or possibly snowing, shortly. I won't allow you to risk trying to make it to the ranch before the storm. It will be dark soon."

"You won't allow...," he broke off laughing. "You sound like Ma. I'll do fine. It isn't that I haven't been out in bad weather before and I've certainly traveled the trail between town and the ranch often enough to know the way."

"Andrew was telling me that you brothers, and other young men from the ranches, often stayed overnight in the livery after a dance— especially if the weather was bad. One evening I convinced him not to strike out for home in a storm, so that's where he stayed, I suppose. He wouldn't let me try to make other arrangements."

"Very well. Is that what you suggest?" he said with a grin. "That I sleep in the livery?"

"In that finery you're wearing?" she said, laughing. "No. You can do better. I'm sure Missus Larson has an extra room available in the boardinghouse. That's certain to be more comfortable, and she serves excellent food. Then tomorrow you can visit again with William. Pick up his spirits. That's often as important to healing as medicine."

"You think the storm will break by morning?"

Her eyebrows lifted quizzically. "You should know more about Montana weather than me. I'm a newcomer. What do you think?"

"I'm not sure. Storms usually last more than one day."

"That's better yet," she said. "Hold off until the weekend and I'll ride out there with you. That way you'll have a couple of days with William."

Henrik nodded. "That might work out. I'm looking forward to seeing the folks, but it won't do any great harm to wait a day or two." Besides, he thought, I'll be spending time with the most beautiful woman in Montana. Nothing could top that.

The wheels of the one-horse buggy tended to splatter mud on its passengers, a reminder of the storm that had passed through. Emily was thankful she had the presence of mind to cover her cloak with an old duster, even though Henrik had provided a lap robe. The idea of wearing her riding clothes, in company with the elegantly dressed man, was not given any consideration at all. She had, in fact, given special attention to her choice of attire. The dress she wore, having only a modest bustle, was of a green that nearly matched her eyes and complimented her reddish-brown hair. Leg-of-mutton sleeves were trimmed with white lace, as was the collar. The wool scarf that covered her head and ears had been selected in deference to climate rather than fashion.

Although the morning had dawned bright and clear, the temperature was below freezing. Henrik was protected from the elements by an elaborately trimmed chesterfield worn over a waistcoat and vest. The bowler hat was still in place but, like his companion, a scarf was used to guard neck and ears against the cool wind.

At some distance from the ranch, they caught sight of several people coming out of the house to watch their approach.

"Bet they're wondering who is bringing the teacher," Henrik said. "They might shoot me if they think it's someone making a play for their sister."

"Well are you?" she said mischievously.

"Of course," he answered. "I'd have to be blind and dumb if I wasn't."

"Oh, you...," she said, feigning irritation that she didn't feel. "I'll bet you tell that to every girl you meet in every port. How many girls does that amount to, anyway?"

He laughed. "Fewer than you think. You should see some of the girls in some of the ports. Ug!"

"Don't tell me that you become particular after many months at sea?"

"At the sight of some of those gals, a feller loses all romantic interest." He looked at the young woman at his side. "Speaking of romance, I don't believe you could honestly tell me that my brothers haven't been showing an interest in you?"

Emily ducked her head and blushed. Then, amused by her reaction, she giggled. "Some, I guess."

"All right," he said. "I suppose there's hope for them yet. Who has the inside track?"

She gave him a look of indignation. "Well, you're a very nosy man. What makes you think I'm interested in any of your brothers?"

"Why not? They're not a bad looking bunch. A bit on the rowdy side at times, but some of the local gals didn't seem to mind having them around—especially Frank. He was the one that got most attention. They were drawn to him like ants to sugar."

She was curious. "Why him so much more than the others?"

"Well, Zach is too sobersided. Gals prefer a feller that's more fun. And Billy, he didn't seem to be interested. He'd rather be around horses. Course he may have changed in the four years I've been away."

She had to ask. "How about Andrew?"

"Puddin' Head?" He laughed. "Puddin' Head was always too shy around the gals. Blushing and stuttering. He was an embarrassment. Don't think he'll ever get a gal interested in him."

"Why not? What makes you an authority about women's likes and dislikes?" Her voice showed her displeasure.

Henrik looked at her sharply. "I'm not, but I remember the gals making fun of him for being so big and slow. He was bigger than me, before I left, and still growing. Must be huge by now."

"He is. But he isn't slow." She sat for a moment, seething, before she spoke again. "Have you ever considered that the reason he received so much teasing was due to that nickname his brothers gave him?"

"You mean Puddin' Head?"

"That's a terrible name," she said. "Why did you call him that?"

"Pa was the one that started it. I remember when it happened." He chuckled with the recollection. "Pudd..., I mean Andrew, ...was only about eight or nine. Ma had made some delicious apple pudding for a Christmas Eve dessert. The little feller was eating it until we thought he'd burst. Four or five helpings. After he'd finished, Pa said, 'all right, Puddin' Head, go bring in some firewood if you can still move.' The whole family laughed, so the name stuck. Is he still called 'Puddin' Head?"

"Not if I have anything to say about it." Her face was set in a grim mask. "Your mother feels the same way, so you'd better be careful."

"I remember," he said as they turned toward the house. "She didn't like it then, but thanks for the warning anyway. Is it all right if I call him Andy? Andrew seems so formal."

"Hey Emily," they heard Franklin shout. "Who's that dude with you?" His grin widened as they pulled to a stop. "Well I'll be damned if it ain't ol' Henny. Didn't recognize you in that bowler derby. Don't you look like a dandy, though?"

Henrik bounded off the carriage and grabbed his brother in a bear hug, swinging him around. Then he reached for Zachary. "How you doing there, ol' hoss?" he said, shaking his sibling's hand. When he turned to Andrew, he stopped cold in his tracks to regard the youngest brother. "My God, man!" he said. "Aren't you ever going to stop growing?" The answer he received was having his bowler hat pounded down around his ears. He laughed and pulled his hat off his head. Then he saw his mother. She had remained standing on the porch and appeared to have her emotions under control, but when her oldest son started up the steps, her composure collapsed and the tears flowed.

"Henrik," she cried, falling into his arms. "Oh Henrik."

He held his mother until her sobbing ceased.

Agnus and her son stood quietly behind. Finally the Indian woman came forward and put her big arms around the pair. "Velkommen hjem, Henrik," she said.

"Agnus!" he said, kissing her on the cheek. Then he looked at the boy. "Is that you, Hagen? Why you was just a little varmint when I left. What happened to you?"

The youth shuffled his feet, embarrassed. "Nothin' much."

Henrik took his mother's face in his hands. "I left William just a couple of hours ago. He's doing much better. Miss O'Neill's father sent a telegram to Doctor Morrison suggesting some treatments that seem to be doing the trick. Billy's already talking about coming home. Of course the doctor said he'd have to wait for a while."

Karen Jones clutched her son and cried happily. A moment passed before she looked at the young woman, still seated on the carriage, and smiled. "Kom kjœre deg," she said. Du tilhører familien."

Tears formed in Emily's eyes when, in her mind, she translated the mother's words: Come dear, you belong with this family.

# 25

"I didn't get shanghaied," Henrik said. "Guess I was lucky."

The family was enjoying the warmth of the big fireplace after dinner. Standing with his back to the blazing logs, the oldest son held court.

Emily was first to pose the question. "What does that mean?"

He smiled at the teacher. "Life on some ships isn't too pleasant—particularly those that carry a lot of sail. Climbing around in the rigging is hard work and dangerous. The pay isn't much and the food is terrible. Lots of sickness and dysentery. A month can go by without ever seeing land. Some fellers can't take it. Desert the first chance they get. That leaves the ship short-handed and since there's not too many standing in line for the jobs, the ship's master will often make up a full crew with some that aren't there entirely by choice." He winked at the teacher.

"Land sakes!" she said, eyes wide. "How do they do that?"

"There are some enterprising gentlemen in San Francisco, and most other big ports, who make a business of supplying ships with crew members. They don't bother looking at the fellers hangin' around the docks. Those boys are there, trying to pick up a quick buck, and they're usually too smart to be caught and sent shipping out. But the bars and boardinghouses are a good source of footloose crackers or clodhoppers or cow chasers like me, who have come to the city lookin' for adventure. They're the easiest to convince about the wondrous life of a sailor, and usually end up in the hold of a ship with a terrible hangover or a knot on the head. By the time the ship has set sail for Shanghai or Singapore or Calcutta, it's too late for them to change their minds. And these voyages often last years."

Emily nodded. "So that's why the word 'shanghai'. Because Shanghai might be their destination. How did you avoid becoming one of those unfortunate men?" she said to the dashing, older Jones brother.

He chuckled. "It wasn't because I was smart. Like I said, lucky. When I hit 'Frisco, I headed for the docks at the foot of Market Street. By chance, a large steam-powered sailing ship, called the Alexandria, was moored there. When I saw that ship, it was like a dream coming true. Wherever it was going, I wanted to go. Maybe it was the name. I'd been reading about Alexandria. That's a city on the Mediterranean side of Egypt. It was originally the capital until they founded Cairo. When they finished the Suez canal in sixty-nine, it became accessible to trading ships from the Pacific or Indian oceans. I wanted to see that city. I still want to, but we haven't been out that far yet. Most of our business is in Australia and southeast Asia.

"Whatever the reason, when I saw that ship I was hooked." He smiled at his mother. "It must be all that Viking blood in my veins. I suppose you could say I shanghaied myself. Went right up to the ship's master and told him I wanted to hire on." Henrik laughed. "He was so surprised, he didn't know what to say, but he took me on."

"How exciting!" Emily said. "Tell us about life aboard a ship. My only knowledge comes from books."

The elder Jones brother showed the teacher a grin. "It isn't all in books. I learned that in a hurry. Like I said before, it's hard work and sometimes dangerous. The ship's master is Olaf Johansen." He glanced at his mother. "Another Norwegian. He took a liking to me—took me under his wing, you could say. Coming off the ranch, I was in good physical condition and I knew how to work. Being able to read and write gave me a leg up. Eventually I was put in charge of the ship's manifest. Looking back, I can see that the captain was grooming me for the first mate's position. He insisted that I learn every sailor's job, starting with the hardest and dirtiest. I shoveled coal in the boilers and oiled the machinery. I also had to learn sails and rigging, so I spent a lot of time aloft."

Franklin interrupted. "Why does the ship have sails if it's steam driven."

"We make long-distance voyages—almost to the other side of the world. If we were powered by steam alone, all our cargo space would be taken up by fuel. And fuel isn't always available at some of our ports of call. Primarily we use the steam to power through doldrums."

"Doldrums?"

"Yeah, Frank. Places where there's no wind."

"Why do you go there?" the brother persisted.

Henrik chuckled. "We don't always know where they are. At times they can be almost anywhere."

"How long have you been first mate?" Emily said.

"Let see..." He lifted his eyes to the ceiling

as he pondered the question. "About thirteen months. There was a lot to learn. Navigation for one thing. I'm still learning. Johansen is pushing me toward getting my master's papers. He wants me to take over for him when he's ready for shore life. His wife is urging him to give it up."

"He's married!" Emily gave the sailor a look of disbelief. "What woman would want to be married to a man she hardly ever sees?"

He showed her a wry grin. "There's some, I guess, but most of the old-timers are married to the sea. I expect that'll be my lot in life."

"Nei!" A small cry escaped Karen Jones which told the teacher that the older woman understood everything being said.

Her oldest son's face reflected the sadness he felt. "Beklager, Mor. Men dette er noe jeg må gjøre."

He's sorry, Emily thought. What a shame. But then, like he told his mother, it's something he must do.

# 26

"Your mother is very disappointed," Emily said. She studied the face of the handsome man that rode William's big gelding alongside. "She's been hoping you would come back and take charge of the ranch operation."

Henrik shook his head. "I know. But I've already found the life I want to lead." He looked around the dismal prairie. "I'd be one unhappy cowboy if I allowed myself to be stuck here for all time."

A blizzard had been blowing across the Montana Territory for several days. It confined the teacher to the ranch and, by unspoken agreement of all concerned, closed the school. The Jones brothers had ventured outdoors only to haul hay and otherwise tend to the stock.

With the storm's passing, Emily had chosen to ride with the older brother to check on the condition of the cattle in the northern sector. Had William been capable, he would have taken this assignment, but today would be his first day at home. Zachary had left early that morning with the buckboard to return the injured young man to his family.

The powder-like snow, blown with the wind, was piled up against anything that presented an obstruction—bushes, embankments or, in a few instances, dead cattle. The same wind swept clear much of the flat surface down to bare earth. Clumps of yellow grass showed here and there.

A high overcast gave the sky a slate gray

cast which barely allowed the yellow sun to penetrate. Emily shivered in her sheepskin-lined coat and pulled her scarf up around her cheeks. The breeze, left over from the storm, was cold.

"I think you'll agree that everyone has a right to take charge of his or her own life. If I remember correctly," Henrik said, with a sidewise glance, "you preferred being a teacher rather than pursue a career in medicine as your father wanted you to do."

Emily gave her companion a smile. "He would have been pleased if I could have become a doctor. We both knew there was next to no chance of that ever happening. Very few women have been allowed to attend medical school. As for any other career in medicine—nursing or whatever—that would have given him no satisfaction. It was doctor or nothing. But he's quite consoled that I chose the teaching profession."

"How long can you put up with this Godforsaken piece of hell on earth?" He looked around and shook his head. "I can't imagine why Pa chose to settle here. The Pacific Northern railroad passes through some fine looking country between here and the west coast. They were headed for Oregon where there's some pretty good farmland. Almost anywhere is better than this."

Emily giggled. "Your mother told me the story of Broken Wagon. That's a charming little tale."

Henrik snorted. "What's not so charming is trying to make a living out here. Most folks give up and move on. Those that's left are a bunch of real stubborn people, like Ma."

The teacher felt the need to defend her employer. "She's certainly done right by your family.  The ranch is very prosperous."

"Well," he said, "I hope so for the sake of her and my brothers, but it's been hard on her."

Emily gave the Jones man a long look. "How about you?  Unless I misunderstood, you own one of the homesteads here."

He laughed.  "That's right, but I sure wouldn't know where to find it.  I think it's over on the south side.  Anyway, I don't think it will be mine for very long."  In answer to the quizzical expression that crossed her face, he went on. "Soon as the government finds out that I'm an absentee owner, they'll probably reclaim it."

"Land sakes!" she said.  "That's a possibility.  It's been more than five years since you filed for the homestead.  You'd better do something about it before you leave."

"What do you suggest?" he said, grinning.

"I'm not certain."  A frown appeared.  "I'll need to ask Andrew about that."

"Andrew?"

"Yes," she told the Jones brother.  "He's taken an interest in law.  My father sent out quite a number of law books and he's been poring over them for the past several months."

"Of course," he said.  "I remember now. Frank was telling me something about Andrew's studies.  "Why law?"

"He thought that knowing something about the law could be useful now that he's taking over management of the ranch."  She felt no need to tell Henrik that it was her idea.  "With Montana about to become a state, we can expect the new congress to pass laws regulating cattle and mining industries.  Washington has been content to keep hands-off so far.  Same with the territorial governor."

He shook his head grinning. "It's hard to believe that ol' Andy has become a bookworm." Glancing around at the barren plains, he suddenly stood up in his stirrups and pointed. "What's that?"

"I don't know," she said squinting. "It looks like a cow."

They turned their horses and galloped toward the mound that disrupted the otherwise flat part of the landscape.

"It is a cow or a steer," he shouted as they drew near. The animal lifted its head and looked at the approaching riders. "Old cow," he said, pulling his horse to a stop, "and nearly frozen to death. Probably figured it was easier just to lay down here and die. I don't know if we can save her. How close are we to one of Andrew's shelters?"

She pointed. "I believe there's one over there near the river."

He nodded. "Think I see it. We'll have to try and get her up on her feet." He shook out his lasso and cast the loop over the animal's horns. "Haven't lost a thing," he told the young woman with a wink. "Now while I pull, you get behind her and slap her on the rump with your rope. Don't be too gentle. We've got to get her moving."

Emily did as she was told while Henrik's horse applied tension to the lariat. The cow slid a few yards before she struggled to her feet. Then, on wobbly legs, she trailed along, in a rather docile manner, behind the big horse. Every time she showed any resistance, Emily swatted her with the rope.

When they reached the shed, they saw cattle outside, feeding on piles of hay that had been off loaded earlier, and a few inside. "Good,"

Henrik said. They'll have the place nice and warm. Might save this ol' girl yet."

The cow was pulled adjacent to the shed opening where she stood, legs splayed. He loosened the lariat until it fell off her horns, then stepped down from the saddle. "Come on," he said, "let's get her inside."

It required a considerable amount of pushing and tail-twisting to get the exhausted animal inside where she stumbled to a vacant corner and collapsed.

Henrik walked out to one of the piles of hay and returned with arms full. "Don't expect her to be much interested in eating," he said, depositing the hay inside, "but it's there if she wants it."

"We've done all we can for her," Henrik said as they remounted. "It's up to her, now."

"Do you think she'll survive?" Emily said.

He shook his head. "Probably not. She's an older cow. But I could be wrong. These longhorns are pretty tough. At least we've given her a chance."


They were eating supper when Emily brought up the matter of Henrik's homestead.

Andrew paused, with his soupspoon in midair, to consider her question. After a moment he lowered the spoon into the bowl and crossed his arms. "In the original Homestead Act, a settler could get around the residency requirement by paying a fee of a buck and a quarter an acre. I'll find out if the fee can be paid later to change the status of the property. However, I doubt that can be done. Another way would be for you to sell your homestead to Ma."

"Nei!" Karen Jones interrupted. "Henrik må beholde noe eiendommen i hans navn.

"Mor," the older brother said gently. "It wouldn't do me any good and it would just complicate matters for you trying to hold on to property in my name."

Andrew had leaned back in his chair, his hands behind his head. "There might be another way," he said. "We could make the ranch a corporation. Henrik could sell his property to the corporation and own shares in proportion to his contribution. Us other brothers can follow suit as soon as the five year terms on our homesteads expire.

"Ma, you could do the same except for this original homestead that has the ranch buildings. You'd want to keep it separate so that you wouldn't lose it if the corporation went bankrupt. After us brothers have divested ourselves of our holdings..."

"Hold on a minute!" Franklin interrupted. Divested ourselves? "That's purdy fancy lingo you're throwin' around here. Is that what you learned outta them law books?"

Andrew grinned at his brother. "Gotcha hornswoggled, don't I? Yup, that comes from the books. In our case it means getting rid of our properties by selling to the corporation. Then I believe we'd be eligible to take out other homesteads on that part of the range we use but don't own. You can't apply for another homestead if you already own one. In seventy-three they changed the law allowing people to file for bigger homesteads. Congress finally decided that a hundred and sixty acres wasn't enough land to support a family in some areas. I have a hunch this is one of those areas. If we continued taking out new homesteads every five years, eventually we'd have clear title to all that range."

"How would you go about getting it done?" Zachary wanted to know.

"Have to wait until the state government is in place," Andrew said. "Then I could apply for a state charter of incorporation. Probably make a trip to Helena to do this. There'd be a fee and we'd need to designate our corporate officers. The family would vote on this, but I expect Ma would be president. Vice-president would be Zachary, since he'd be the oldest brother in residence and I'd be the secretary and treasurer because I'm the only one who reads law books...," he sneered at Franklin, "...and knows what he's doing."

More laughter followed after Henrik told his brother, "Frank, we'll vote you in as court jester." The younger brother suddenly stood and grabbed his sibling in a headlock while rubbing his knuckles on the other's scalp. "I quit! I quit!" Henrik pleaded.

"Franklin!" the smiling mother said in halfhearted admonishment. "Du må opptøre deg!"

The number three son grinned at his mother and took his seat. "I'll behave if you make him stop picking on me."

"One more thing," Andrew said after the brothers had settled down. "We'd need a name for our corporation."

"I know," William said. Everyone looked in surprise at the reserved man, who sat in an easy chair near the table and hadn't uttered a word all evening. "The Jones Cattle Company."

"Tricky name," Henrik said dryly.

"I like it," Zachary told the group.

Karen Jones nodded.

"Hold on a minute!" Franklin said. "I'd like

to know how I'd be better off having shares in a corporation than I would be as someone who owns separate land?"

"I don't know, Frank," Andrew scratched his head. How much are you getting from your little hundred and sixty acres? How many head of cattle are raised on your property? What's your income? Can you answer that?"

"Income?" the other said. "You mean wages? We don't get no wages. You know that. When we need money, Ma gives it to us. Only one gets wages is Emily." He grinned at the teacher.

"Wouldn't you like to know what your actual earnings should be?" the big man said. "The corporation would pay you a salary for your work. Dividends from profit sharing would be added to that and you'd have your investment grow as time passes. I believe we're going to see this ranch become one of the largest in Montana and you'd be a part of that."

"Count me in, "Zachary said.

"Me too," said William.

"How about you, Ma?" Franklin asked his mother.

"Ya, det er bra."

"You, Henny?"

"Sure," the brother replied. "I've got nothing to lose."

"Well, what the hell!" Franklin said. "May as well go along for the ride."

"Would you welcome one more investor?" All heads turned to look at Emily. "I'd like to file on one of those homesteads, if you'd approve."

Henrik was the first to begin clapping and was quickly joined by the others. "I can't imagine an investor we'd rather have in the corporation," he said.

Andrew was grinning from ear to ear. "I thought you said you weren't interested in applying for a homestead."

"Well!" she said haughtily. "A lady can change her mind."

# 27

Emily was standing on the walkway in front of the Broken Wagon bank when she saw Henrik's rented rig coming into town. Karen Jones, sitting ramrod straight on the buggy seat, accompanied her oldest son. The teacher rushed out in the street to meet the two. "Did you hear the news?" she said, her face flushed with excitement. "It's happened. Montana has been admitted to the Union—the forty-first state. Isn't it thrilling?"

Henrik and his mother looked around at the town's citizens who were smiling, shaking hands and bantering cheerfully. "When did this happen?" he said.

"Yesterday, eighth of November. Telegram came in today. They're saying that Joseph K. Toole will most likely be the governor."

"Never heard of him," the Jones man said. Then he grinned. "Why aren't you in school? Are you playing hooky?"

Emily giggled. "The students have been excused. Mister Petersen came up to my classroom and told me that the town council has decided to declare today a holiday. There'll be a celebration and a dance tonight. Mister Jensen has printed bulletins to be posted around town and sent out to all the ranches. We're fortunate that the weather is moderate for this time of year so that most folks will be able to come."

"You're going to the dance, aren't you?" Henrik knew he had never seen a woman more lovely than the one standing before him. She was fairly sparkling.

"I wouldn't miss it," she told him, "and I expect all five of my boyfriends to be there, along with their mother. You'd better hurry back to the ranch and get everyone all gussied up."

Karen Jones blushed and waved her hand. "Nei. Jeg kan ikke gå," she said shyly.

"Oh yes you will!" the teacher said sternly. "This is the most important event to ever take place in this part of the country, and you're going to attend if I have to come and drag you here by the hair. Now, should we go shopping or do you have everything you need?"

Henrik was dumfounded. He had never heard anyone speak to his mother in that manner. His astonishment increased when the older woman climbed down from the buggy and meekly took the teachers arm. "Ja," she said. "Vi gå."

"I'm so happy that this happened while you were here," she said to the extraordinarily good-looking man that swung her around the dance floor. She knew that the eyes of every woman in the place was fixed on her partner. "When will you be leaving for Seattle?"

"I received the answer to my telegram today," Henrik said. "Captain Johansen wants me there by the twenty-seventh. I'll be going down to Billings day after tomorrow."

"Oh," she said, disappointed. "So soon?"

"It's time." He showed her a smile. "I'm getting a terrible urge for the taste of sea water. Besides," he said, pulling her close and whispering in her ear, "the longer I'm around you

187

the more difficult it will be for me to go."

Blushing, she pushed him away—but not too much. "Silly," she said. "I imagine you'll be spending all your time thinking of me when you're with an alluring girl in one of those exotic places."

"I wouldn't be surprised," he said, half seriously.

"Oh you!" She decided to retreat to a more safe discussion. "Has your ship been repaired."

Henrik chuckled and took the hint. "Nearly. The replacement parts finally arrived. Had to come by rail from back east."

"That must have been a bad storm to have caused so much damage."

His face became thoughtful. "The worst I've ever seen. Even with everything reefed, we still lost two masts."

"Were you frightened?" she said.

"Of course not," he told her with a grin. "Stout-hearted men never get frightened. Just because I lost my dinner a few times, doesn't mean I was scared."

She laughed. "No. I wouldn't think you were. But you're ready to go out and do it again?"

"Well, no one ever said sailors were smart."

The music stopped and he stood holding her hand. "So tell me, and be honest. What are your plans. Will you be going back to New York soon?"

She showed him a devious little grin. "Can that question wait until later? I promise I'll let you know."

"Oh," he said, eyebrows lifted. "When is later? Am I to expect an announcement of some kind?"

"I wouldn't call it that, but right now I'm not sure. Just be patient. I might have an answer before the celebration is over."

"Well, in that case," he said, leading her off the dance floor, "we'd better join the brothers. They're looking rather anxious over there. Probably think I'm trying to keep you for myself."

"I'm not very good at this," Zachary said. "You should be dancin' with Frank. He's the dandy of the family."

Emily laughed. "He's on my list, but I think it will be quite a bit later. There's a flock of young ladies clustered around him at the moment."

"That's usually the case. Oops! Beg pardon." He apologized for stepping on her foot. "You're takin' a risk tryin' to get me to dance. I was born with two left feet."

"You're doing fine," she told him, "and you didn't hurt my foot. After you get a little more practice you'll be a good dancer."

"I wouldn't put too much down on that bet if I was you," Zachary said. "I'm kinda awkward around ladies. Except you," he added. "You're easy to be with."

"That's because I've been around for quite a while. Like a sister," she said thoughtfully.

"I'm afraid I can't think of you as a sister." His face reddened with the remark. "Whoa! I shouldn't be sayin' that."

She giggled. "Of course you should. That's what ladies like to hear. I believe you could give Franklin a run for his money if you put your mind to it."

"Nope," he said. "Me and Billy and Andy, we don't handle ourselves too well around the gals. I reckon Ma's gonna have a bunch of bachelors on her hands, except for Frank. And now Henny has takin' hisself out of the runnin'."

She showed him a frown. "You can't make me believe that. You're all too good-looking for the young ladies to leave you alone for very long. Whether you like it or not, each of you is considered to be a prize catch around here. I know. I've heard talk. You just don't make yourself available."

As Ike and Clarence finished playing My Old Kentucky Home and reached for their glasses, Emily disengaged herself from her partner. "Now then," she said, turning the man around and giving him a shove, "go over there and give one of those young ladies a chance."

Emily was grabbed by the arm as she started to leave the dance floor. "I think this is my dance," Franklin said.

She giggled and consulted an imaginary listing. "Oh yes, I have you shown as next on my dance card."

"Well it's about time." He put on a serious face. "I've been waitin' for more than a year—ever' since that time Andy did the fandango with Bull Bjornson and his brothers."

"That was awful," she said. "After that, I had no interest in going to the dances—until tonight."

"Was you worried 'bout causin' another fight?'

"Oh no. I believe Mister Bjornson learned his lesson. That poor man. Is he here tonight? I should give him his dance after the thrashing he took. If he's sober," she added.

Franklin looked around the hall. "I ain't seen him, but if he's here, he ain't sober. By the way," he said, nodding toward his retreating brother.   "What happened between you and Zach?"

"Oh that," she said smiling.   "I just gave him a good talking to about being so shy around girls and sent him over to get acquainted with one of those girls next to the wall."

"He won't do it," Franklin said, "but that answers one question."

"What's that?"  A small frown appeared.

"That tells me Zach's out of the picture."

Emily's face showed puzzlement.   "I don't know what you mean?"

He grinned.   "Remember that time I asked you which of us brothers you'd be marryin'?"

"Yes," she said.   "On the way out to the ranch that first time.  I told you I wouldn't marry anyone here in Montana, or something like that."

"You said it wasn't in your plans, and I said that Ma had other ideas."  His grin spread into a smile.   "Now watchin' you send ol' Zach into the arms of another woman, I know it ain't him.  And with Henny out of the race, that narrows down the field.  In that case, it must be me."

"What?" she said and burst out laughing. At that moment the music started again.  He took her in his arms and they began waltzing to the strains of Home On the Range.   She leaned backward to look in his face.  "You certainly have a high opinion of yourself.   Why would I be marrying you?"

"Why not?" he said.   "I'm likable.   Work hard.   Don't smell too bad or snore too loud. Andy says I'm goin' to be rich and I get along fine with ladies."

"That's what would worry me," she told him.  "You get along too fine with ladies."

"Well, maybe," he said, chuckling.   "But I

191

could be honest, loyal and true as an old hound dog with the right woman."

She showed a skeptical face. "Of course you would, and the right woman would probably come along every five minutes."

"You don't like me," he said with a sad face. "Do you?"

She gave him a quick, fierce hug. "I love you, Franklin," she said, "but I'm certainly not going to marry you."

"Wait a minute!" he said, taken aback. "If you love me why wouldn't you marry me."

"I love your whole family." She giggled at his expression. "I'm not going to marry your whole family."

He was confused. "Does that mean you'd marry part of my family? Which part? What did you and Henrik talk about?"

"I'll tell you later." She gazed past his shoulder and her eyes widened. "Look there!" she said, "and tell me I'm not seeing what I'm seeing."

He turned around. "My god! Ma! She's dancin' with Henry Cotter! She hates Cotter!"

"She can't hate him very much, "Emily said. "See there! She's smiling!"

He shook his head. "If she was liquored up I could understand, but she don't drink. What do you think this means?"

A dozen possibilities flooded their minds and they continued dancing in silence until the music stopped.


"William, how are you feeling?" Emily pulled a vacant chair next to his and sat. "You're not getting too tired, are you?"

"I'm fine," he said, holding up a glass.

"Andy is takin' care of me."

The teacher had seen the Jones brother when he entered the hall, helped by Zachary and Franklin.    Karen Jones, wearing a worried expression, followed close behind.    William's sallow complexion gave evidence of his discomfort.

"The ride was a little rough on him," Franklin had explained while assisting his brother to a chair, "but he insisted on comin' in."

Emily had offered to find doctor Morrision, but William pleaded with her not to do that.    "I don't want people lookin' at me."

"Whatever is in that glass must be helping," she said.    You're looking better than when you came in."

"Wouldn't miss this for the world and I'm feelin' a lot better."    He showed her a brave smile. "I reckon there's still some infection in me. Gettin' stronger, but it's slow comin'."

"Well I'm not going to let them take you home tonight," she said.    "I'll make arrangements with Missus Larson for you to stay at the boarding house.    Then you should see the doctor in the morning.    It might be better if you rested for a couple of days before you go home."

He grinned.    "You're actin' like a mother hen, but you're too late.    Ma already talked with Missus Larson about me and her stayin' there. The brothers will sleep in the livery if she doesn't have enough room for ever'buddy.    We brought bedrolls along."

On an impulse the teacher reached out to feel his forehead, but he pulled away and looked around quickly.    "Don't!    Folks will think I'm sick."

"Don't be silly," she said.    "I just wondered

193

if you had a fever.  I didn't mean to cause you any embarrassment.  Oh, here comes Andrew."

The big man approached carrying two glasses.  He handed one to his brother and turned to Emily.  "Can I get you something to drink?"

"What are you drinking?" she said.

He held up his glass.  "You don't want this. It has whisky in it.  I can get you a soda."

"Is that what you're giving to William? Whisky?"

"Just a little," he said.  "It's mostly water."

"Let me taste."  She reached for his glass and made a face after taking a sip.  "That's awful. Why do you want to drink that?"

He grinned at the young woman.  "Wish I knew."

William mixed the contents of the two glasses he held and handed the empty to his brother.

Andrew toasted his brother.  "Here's to a long life without horns."

"Hear, hear," the other answered.

"You men!" Emily said.  Then to William, "I wouldn't think that liquor is agreeable with your infection.  You really shouldn't have any more."

"Last one," the young man said, holding up the glass.

"You also," she told Andrew.  "We're going to dance and I don't want you falling all over me."

"You're goin' to dance with Andy?"  William looked from one to the other.  "This I've got to see, but now wait a minute!"  He looked at the teacher.  "You'll have danced with all my brothers, except me."

"When you're well, I'll dance ten times with you at the first opportunity," she said smiling.

"No!" His face darkened with irritation. "That's not good enough. I've got to dance with you tonight. This is the big celebration. I want to celebrate too." He looked at his younger brother. "Help me up."

Emily was uncertain. "Do you think that's wise?"

"I want to dance with you. They're playin' Way Down Upon the Swanee River. I can keep up with that. Help me, Andy."

Andrew looked at his teacher and shrugged. The two lifted William from the chair where he stood swaying for a moment. Then he reached for Emily and began a shuffling slow dance. She held him close so he could keep his balance. He seemed to grow stronger as the dance continued and when he turned, Andrew saw a beaming smile on his face.

"You dance quite well," she whispered in his ear. "Who's the lucky girl that's been your partner?"

"Ain't never danced any," he said, "'til now."

"You're teasing," she said. "Of course you have."

"Nope."

"Well," she gave him a squeeze, "from now on you'd better. There's a number of young ladies over there that are wishing some handsome fellow would ask them to dance. Next time I expect to see you out on the floor making their dreams come true." Emily leaned backward to look at her partner and saw that he was blushing furiously. She laughed and kissed him on the cheek.

When the music stopped, he led her to her chair and, in a formal manner, thanked her for the dance.

"Your turn," she said to the big man.

Andrew gave a start when he heard her statement. "I don't know how to dance."

"You're never going to learn younger," Emily told him. She reached for his hand. "Come now."

"Hold on a minute," he said, drawing back his hand. "Let's wait for something slower."

Ike and Clarence were playing Turkey In the Straw.

She saw the determination on his face. "Oh you silly..., all right, but let's step outside for some air. It's getting warm in here. Besides, I want to have a talk with you about something important."

After they had retrieved their coats, she took his arm and they walked out into the crisp November air. As they strolled under a bright moon, he wondered what she had to say of significance.

"There's something I haven't told you." she began. "I wrote to my father a while back. I had a question and the day before yesterday I received his answer in a telegram. In my letter I told him about a very bright young man whom I felt would be a perfect candidate for matriculating into the Harvard law school."

A frown showed on Andrew's face. "Harvard? Where's that?"

"Cambridge, Massachusetts. I told my father you'd made great progress in reading the law in those books he'd sent."

"Massachu...," he shook his head. "I couldn't go there..., it's too far..."

"You must," she said. "It's been arranged. A close personal friend of my father is acquainted with Charles William Eliot. He's the president of Harvard. They're willing to accept you. This is the chance of a lifetime. You simply can't afford to pass it up. And you will be back here during the summers."

"But why should I want to be a lawyer?" Andrew shook his head, stunned. "I'm just a rancher."

"Because Montana needs you. Most of those men who will be elected and appointed to the government offices, are uneducated. You're a man who can make a difference. You can help the government and you can help the ranchers in this state. That means you'd be helping your family and the other folks around Broken Wagon." She looked up into his face. "You'd want to do that, wouldn't you?"

"But then I couldn't live here." His face showed distress.

"No, You'd live in Helena. The capital. But why would you want to live here?"

"This is my home," he said. Then added quietly, "and you're here." He blushed and turned away.

She put her arms around him and pressed herself to his back. "But I won't be here forever. Oh I'll stay around to teach and manage the ranch until you graduate." She chuckled. "And I may be able to teach one of your brothers enough that he can take over management of the ranch. But then I'll be gone."

"Back to New York," he said with resignation.

"I'll be going back there soon, but that will be temporary. Just long enough to get married. My mother would kill me if she couldn't arrange a big, elaborate wedding."

"Wedding?" he croaked. "Married? Who?"

"Who do you think, you big dummy?" She tightened her arms around him.

It took him a while, but then he spun around. A grin spread across his face. "Me? You want to marry me?"

The look on his face brought tears to her eyes. She nodded.

"Me!" He wrapped his arms around her, lifting her off the ground and whirled her around. Then he set her back down and eyed her suspiciously. "Why me? I'm nothing."

"That's not true," she said. "You're my best friend and my hero. It's been that way almost from the beginning. You've been my knight in shining armor, riding to my rescue on a white horse. You've slain the dragon and been the champion defending my honor. All the things that silly, romantic young girls read and dream about. I thought I was too worldly and wise to be taken in by those ridiculous notions, but I'm not."

He started to speak, but she put her hand over his mouth. "Let me say this now, or I may never have the courage later. I want to marry you because you've shown me love like I've never known before. Yes, I know you've loved me from the first time we met." A giggle escaped her. "Your feelings for me weren't very well disguised. There is nothing more precious to a woman than to know she is thoroughly and completely loved without guile or reservations. I want to be with you for the rest of my life and bask in that love."

She paused for a moment. "There's something else you should know. I've been denying my love for you for a long time because I had convinced myself that I didn't want to spend the rest of my life in Montana. I finally realized that it wasn't important where I lived as much as with whom I was living. I want to be with you whether you're here in Broken Wagon, or in

Helena, or in the District of Columbia."

"Washington?" he said. "Why would I be in Washington?"

"Because," she explained sweetly, "That's where a senator, representing the great state of Montana, would be living. Don't look so shocked, dear. You'll get used to the idea.

"Now then," she linked her arm in his, "lets go tell the family I proposed and you accepted. Then we'll have our dance."